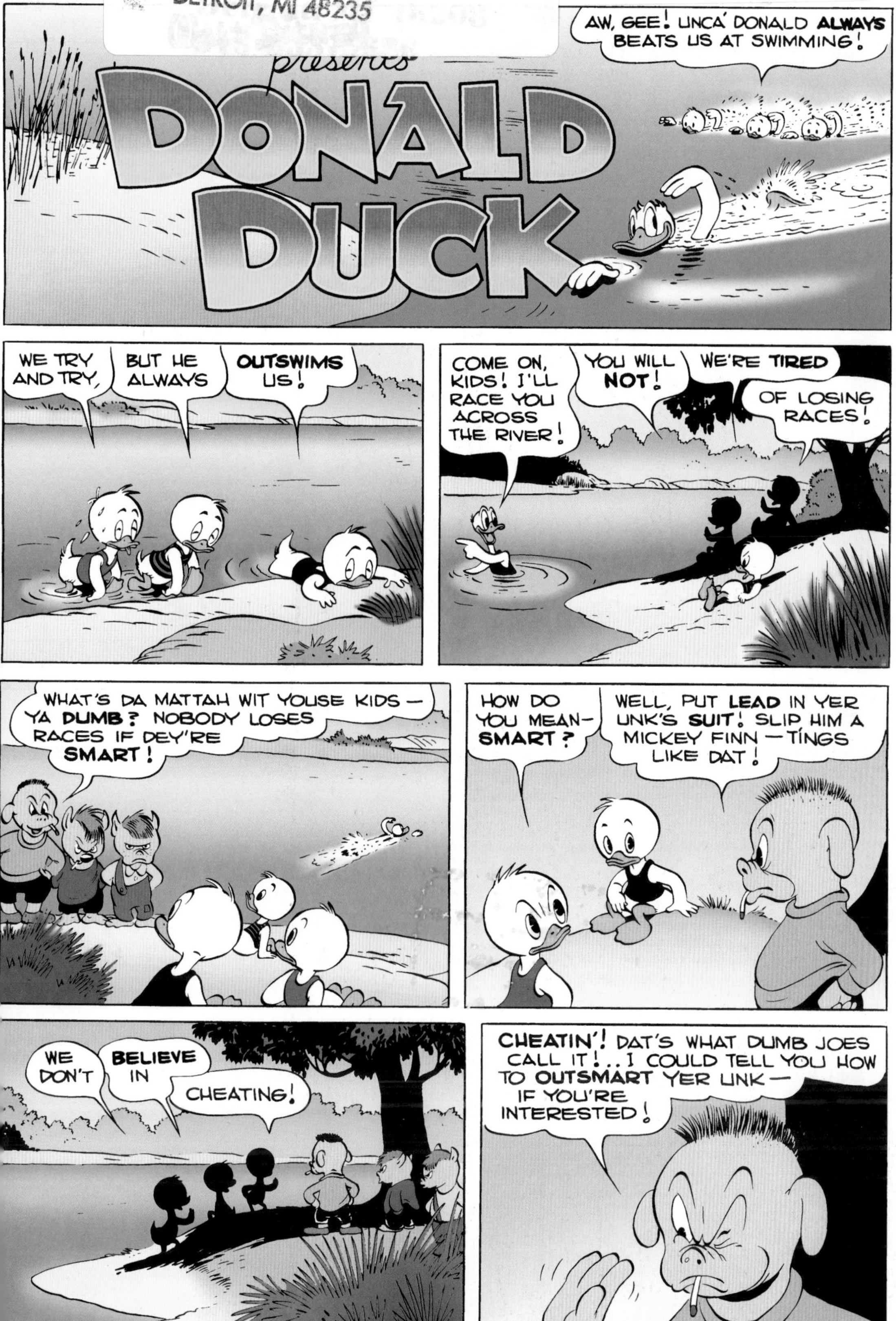
presents
DONALD DUCK
AW, GEE! UNCA' DONALD ALWAYS BEATS US AT SWIMMING!
WE TRY AND TRY,
BUT HE ALWAYS
OUTSWIMS US!
COME ON, KIDS! I'LL RACE YOU ACROSS THE RIVER!
YOU WILL NOT!
WE'RE TIRED
OF LOSING RACES!
WHAT'S DA MATTAH WIT YOUSE KIDS — YA DUMB? NOBODY LOSES RACES IF DEY'RE SMART!
HOW DO YOU MEAN- SMART?
WELL, PUT LEAD IN YER UNK'S SUIT! SLIP HIM A MICKEY FINN — TINGS LIKE DAT!
WE DON'T
BELIEVE IN
CHEATING!
CHEATIN'! DAT'S WHAT DUMB JOES CALL IT!.. I COULD TELL YOU HOW TO OUTSMART YER UNK — IF YOU'RE INTERESTED!

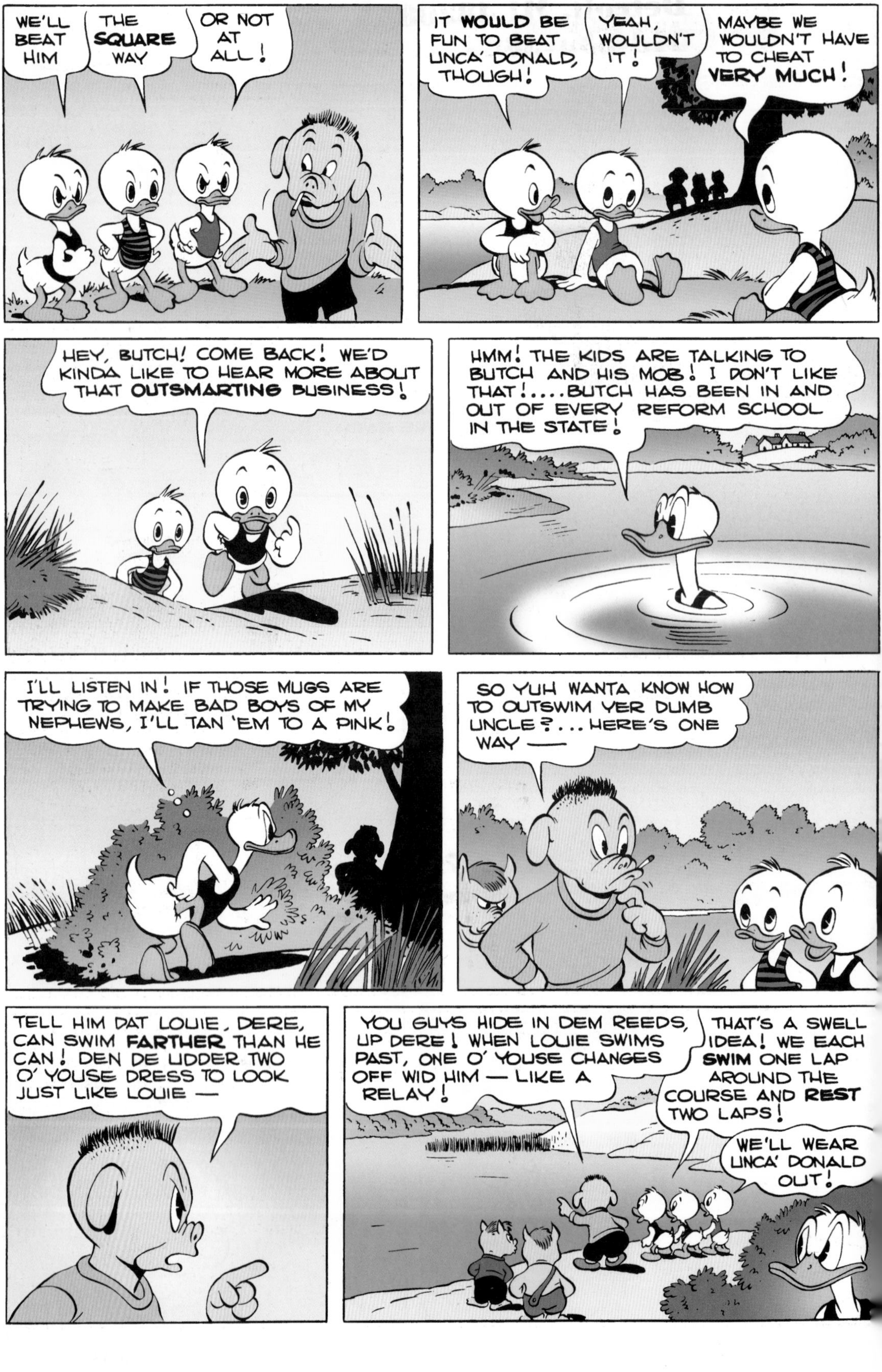
WE'LL BEAT HIM
THE SQUARE WAY
OR NOT AT ALL!
IT WOULD BE FUN TO BEAT UNCA' DONALD, THOUGH!
YEAH, WOULDN'T IT!
MAYBE WE WOULDN'T HAVE TO CHEAT VERY MUCH!
HEY, BUTCH! COME BACK! WE'D KINDA LIKE TO HEAR MORE ABOUT THAT OUTSMARTING BUSINESS!
HMM! THE KIDS ARE TALKING TO BUTCH AND HIS MOB! I DON'T LIKE THAT!....BUTCH HAS BEEN IN AND OUT OF EVERY REFORM SCHOOL IN THE STATE!
I'LL LISTEN IN! IF THOSE MUGS ARE TRYING TO MAKE BAD BOYS OF MY NEPHEWS, I'LL TAN 'EM TO A PINK!
SO YUH WANTA KNOW HOW TO OUTSWIM YER DUMB UNCLE?... HERE'S ONE WAY —
TELL HIM DAT LOUIE, DERE, CAN SWIM FARTHER THAN HE CAN! DEN DE UDDER TWO O' YOUSE DRESS TO LOOK JUST LIKE LOUIE —
YOU GUYS HIDE IN DEM REEDS, UP DERE! WHEN LOUIE SWIMS PAST, ONE O' YOUSE CHANGES OFF WID HIM — LIKE A RELAY!
THAT'S A SWELL IDEA! WE EACH SWIM ONE LAP AROUND THE COURSE AND REST TWO LAPS!
WE'LL WEAR UNCA' DONALD OUT!

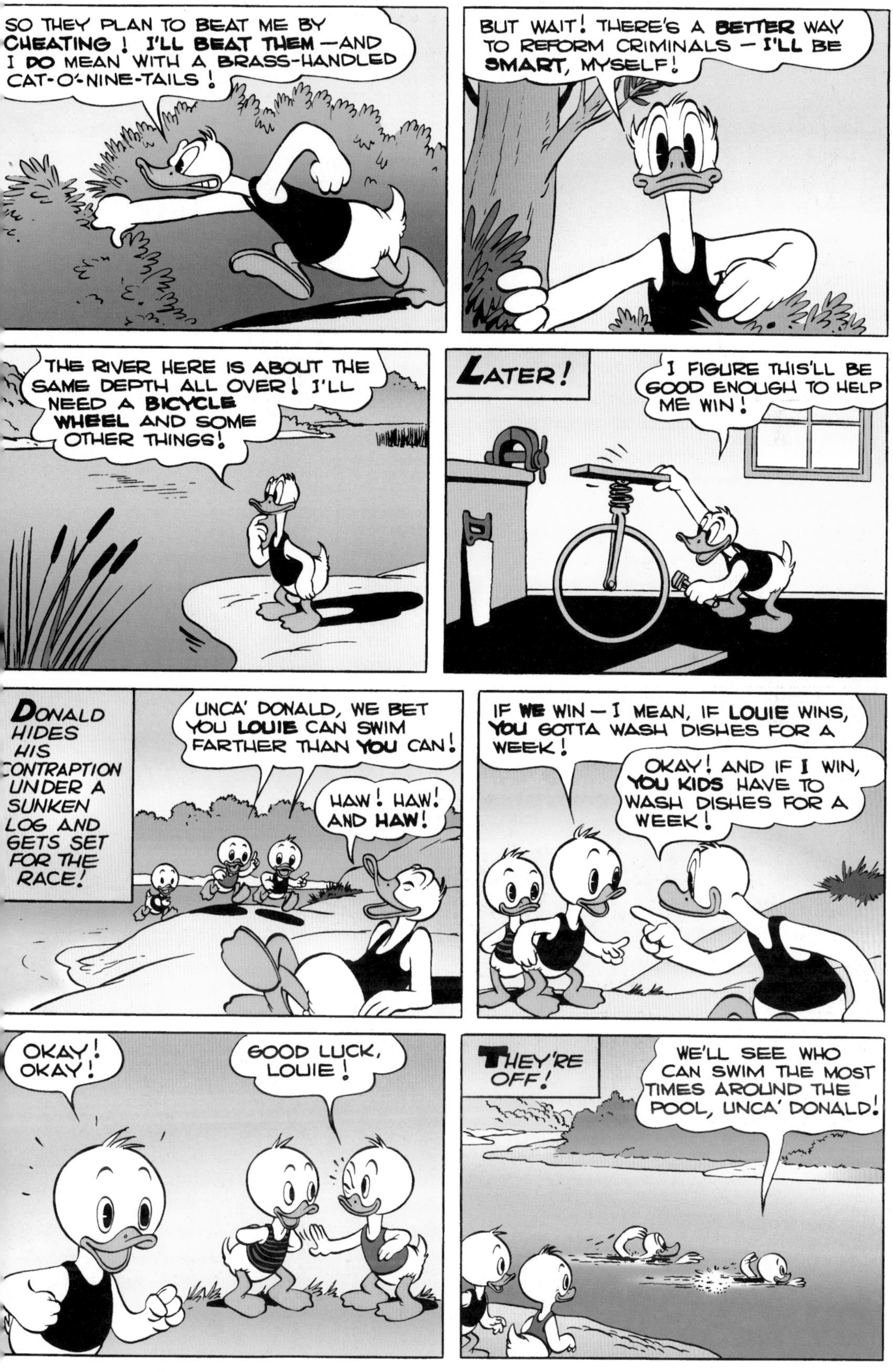
SO THEY PLAN TO BEAT ME BY CHEATING! I'LL BEAT THEM—AND I DO MEAN WITH A BRASS-HANDLED CAT-O'-NINE-TAILS!
BUT WAIT! THERE'S A BETTER WAY TO REFORM CRIMINALS—I'LL BE SMART, MYSELF!
THE RIVER HERE IS ABOUT THE SAME DEPTH ALL OVER! I'LL NEED A BICYCLE WHEEL AND SOME OTHER THINGS!
LATER!
I FIGURE THIS'LL BE GOOD ENOUGH TO HELP ME WIN!
DONALD HIDES HIS CONTRAPTION UNDER A SUNKEN LOG AND GETS SET FOR THE RACE!
UNCA' DONALD, WE BET YOU LOUIE CAN SWIM FARTHER THAN YOU CAN!
HAW! HAW! AND HAW!
IF WE WIN—I MEAN, IF LOUIE WINS, YOU GOTTA WASH DISHES FOR A WEEK!
OKAY! AND IF I WIN, YOU KIDS HAVE TO WASH DISHES FOR A WEEK!
OKAY! OKAY!
GOOD LUCK, LOUIE!
THEY'RE OFF!
WE'LL SEE WHO CAN SWIM THE MOST TIMES AROUND THE POOL, UNCA' DONALD!

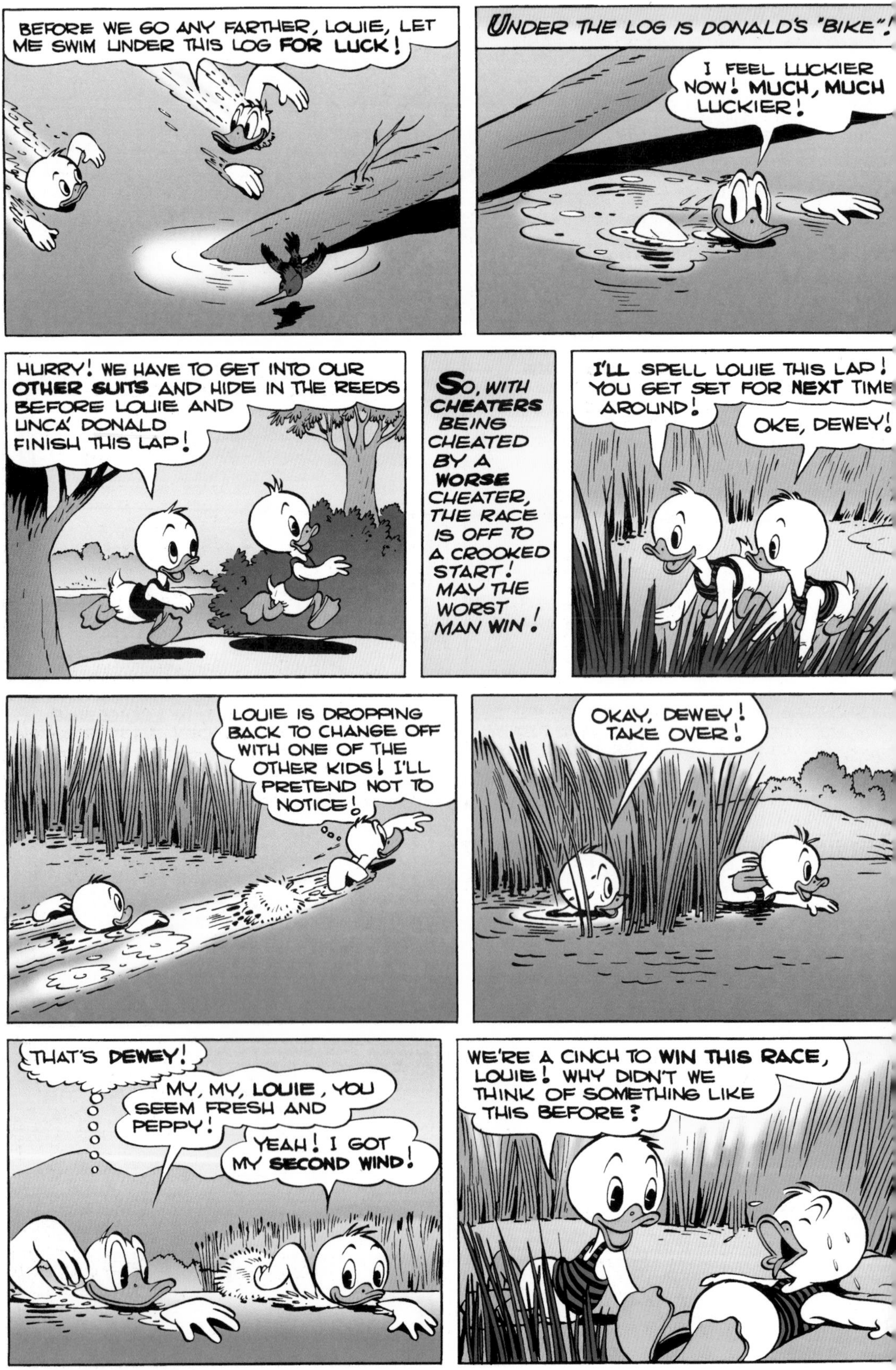

BEFORE WE GO ANY FARTHER, LOUIE, LET ME SWIM UNDER THIS LOG FOR LUCK!
UNDER THE LOG IS DONALD'S "BIKE"!
I FEEL LUCKIER NOW! MUCH, MUCH LUCKIER!
HURRY! WE HAVE TO GET INTO OUR OTHER SUITS AND HIDE IN THE REEDS BEFORE LOUIE AND UNCA' DONALD FINISH THIS LAP!
SO, WITH CHEATERS BEING CHEATED BY A WORSE CHEATER, THE RACE IS OFF TO A CROOKED START! MAY THE WORST MAN WIN!
I'LL SPELL LOUIE THIS LAP! YOU GET SET FOR NEXT TIME AROUND!
OKE, DEWEY!
LOUIE IS DROPPING BACK TO CHANGE OFF WITH ONE OF THE OTHER KIDS! I'LL PRETEND NOT TO NOTICE!
OKAY, DEWEY! TAKE OVER!
THAT'S DEWEY!
MY, MY, LOUIE, YOU SEEM FRESH AND PEPPY!
YEAH! I GOT MY SECOND WIND!
WE'RE A CINCH TO WIN THIS RACE, LOUIE! WHY DIDN'T WE THINK OF SOMETHING LIKE THIS BEFORE?

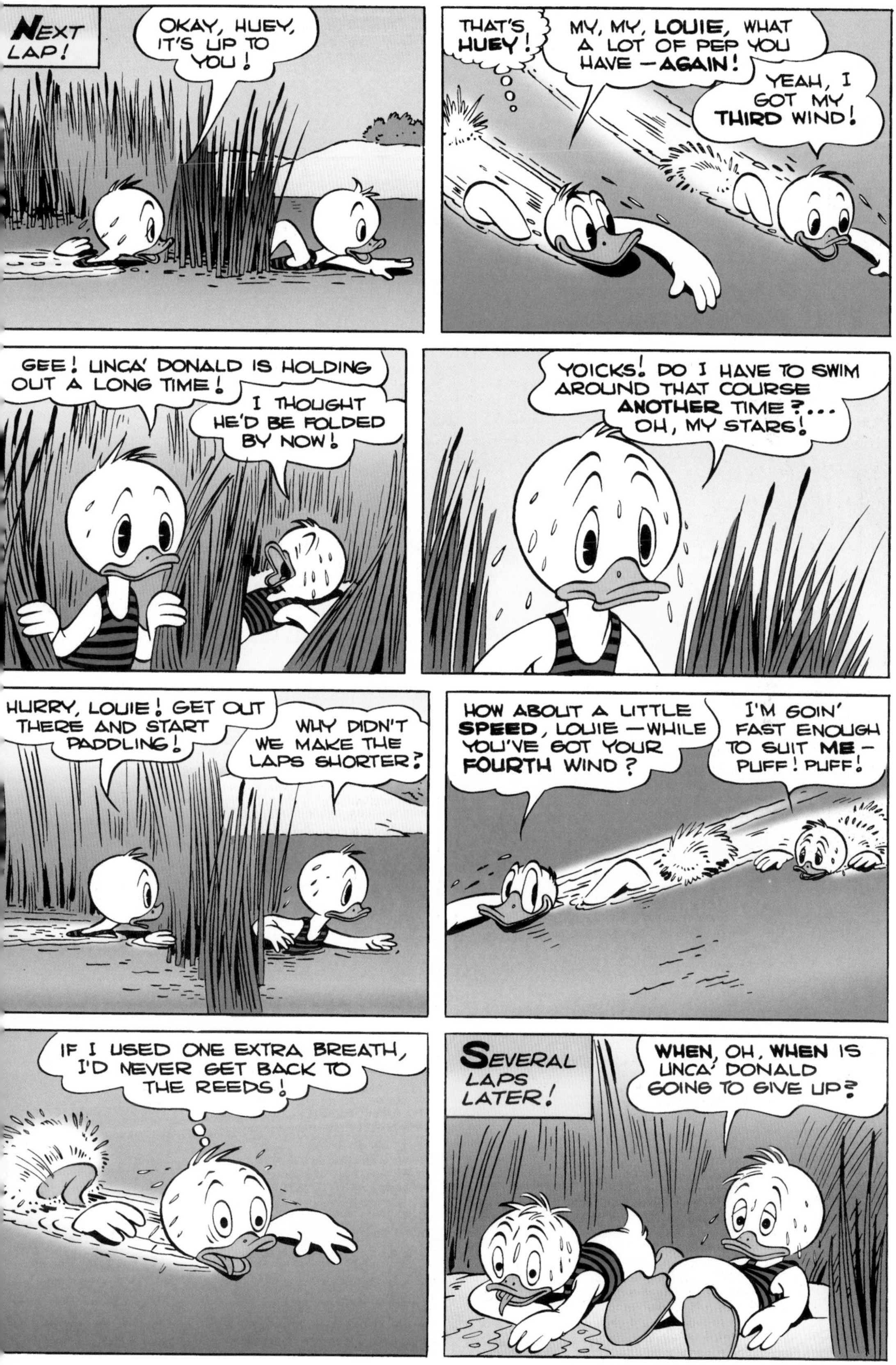
NEXT LAP!
OKAY, HUEY, IT'S UP TO YOU!
THAT'S HUEY!
MY, MY, LOUIE, WHAT A LOT OF PEP YOU HAVE—AGAIN!
YEAH, I GOT MY THIRD WIND!
GEE! UNCA' DONALD IS HOLDING OUT A LONG TIME!
I THOUGHT HE'D BE FOLDED BY NOW!
YOICKS! DO I HAVE TO SWIM AROUND THAT COURSE ANOTHER TIME?... OH, MY STARS!
HURRY, LOUIE! GET OUT THERE AND START PADDLING!
WHY DIDN'T WE MAKE THE LAPS SHORTER?
HOW ABOUT A LITTLE SPEED, LOUIE—WHILE YOU'VE GOT YOUR FOURTH WIND?
I'M GOIN' FAST ENOUGH TO SUIT ME—PUFF! PUFF!
IF I USED ONE EXTRA BREATH, I'D NEVER GET BACK TO THE REEDS!
SEVERAL LAPS LATER!
WHEN, OH, WHEN IS UNCA' DONALD GOING TO GIVE UP?

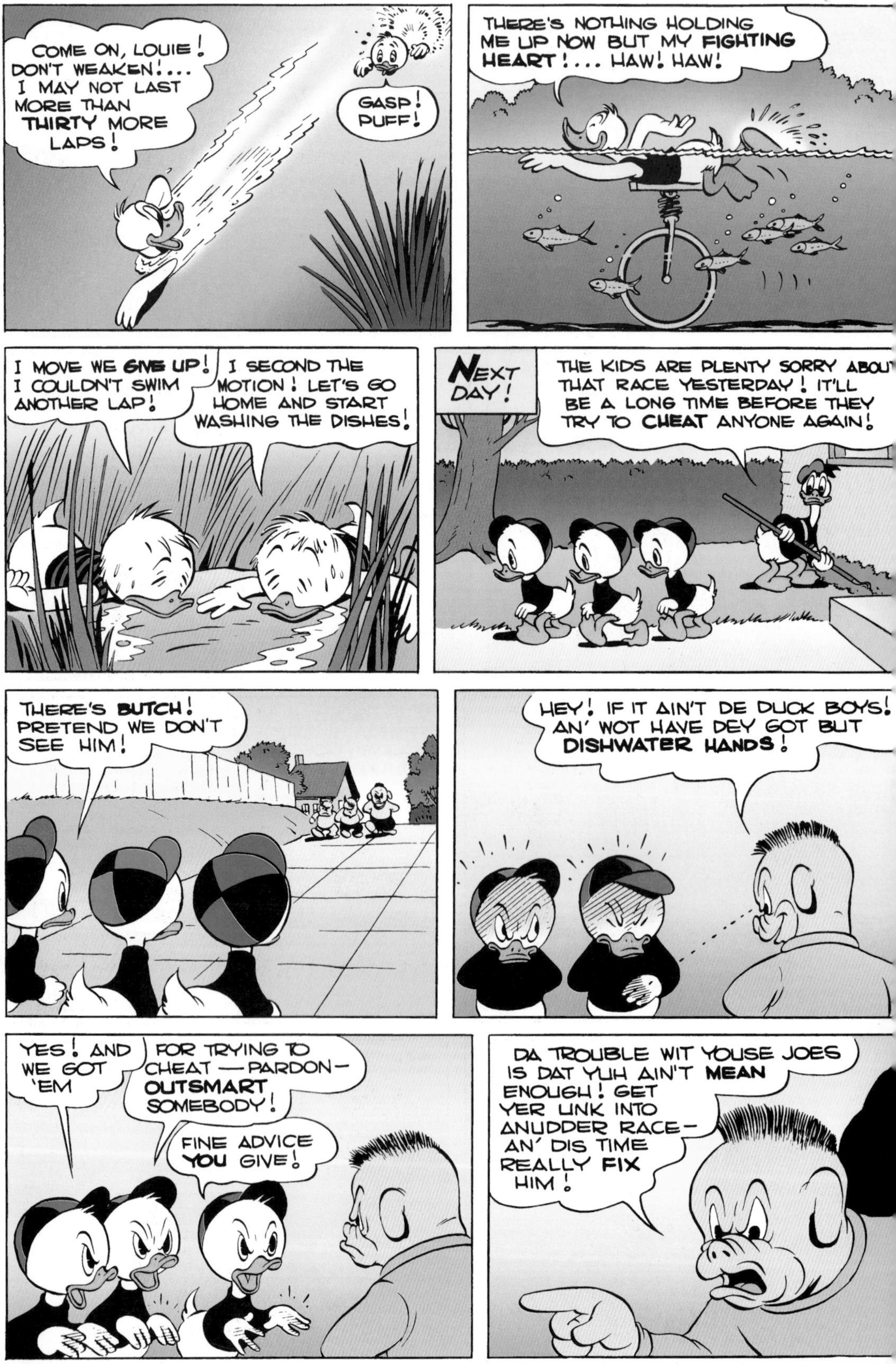
COME ON, LOUIE! DON'T WEAKEN!... I MAY NOT LAST MORE THAN THIRTY MORE LAPS!
GASP! PUFF!
THERE'S NOTHING HOLDING ME UP NOW BUT MY FIGHTING HEART!... HAW! HAW!
I MOVE WE GIVE UP! I COULDN'T SWIM ANOTHER LAP!
I SECOND THE MOTION! LET'S GO HOME AND START WASHING THE DISHES!
NEXT DAY!
THE KIDS ARE PLENTY SORRY ABOUT THAT RACE YESTERDAY! IT'LL BE A LONG TIME BEFORE THEY TRY TO CHEAT ANYONE AGAIN!
THERE'S BUTCH! PRETEND WE DON'T SEE HIM!
HEY! IF IT AIN'T DE DUCK BOYS! AN' WOT HAVE DEY GOT BUT DISHWATER HANDS!
YES! AND WE GOT 'EM
FOR TRYING TO CHEAT — PARDON — OUTSMART SOMEBODY!
FINE ADVICE YOU GIVE!
DA TROUBLE WIT YOUSE JOES IS DAT YUH AIN'T MEAN ENOUGH! GET YER LINK INTO ANUDDER RACE— AN' DIS TIME REALLY FIX HIM!

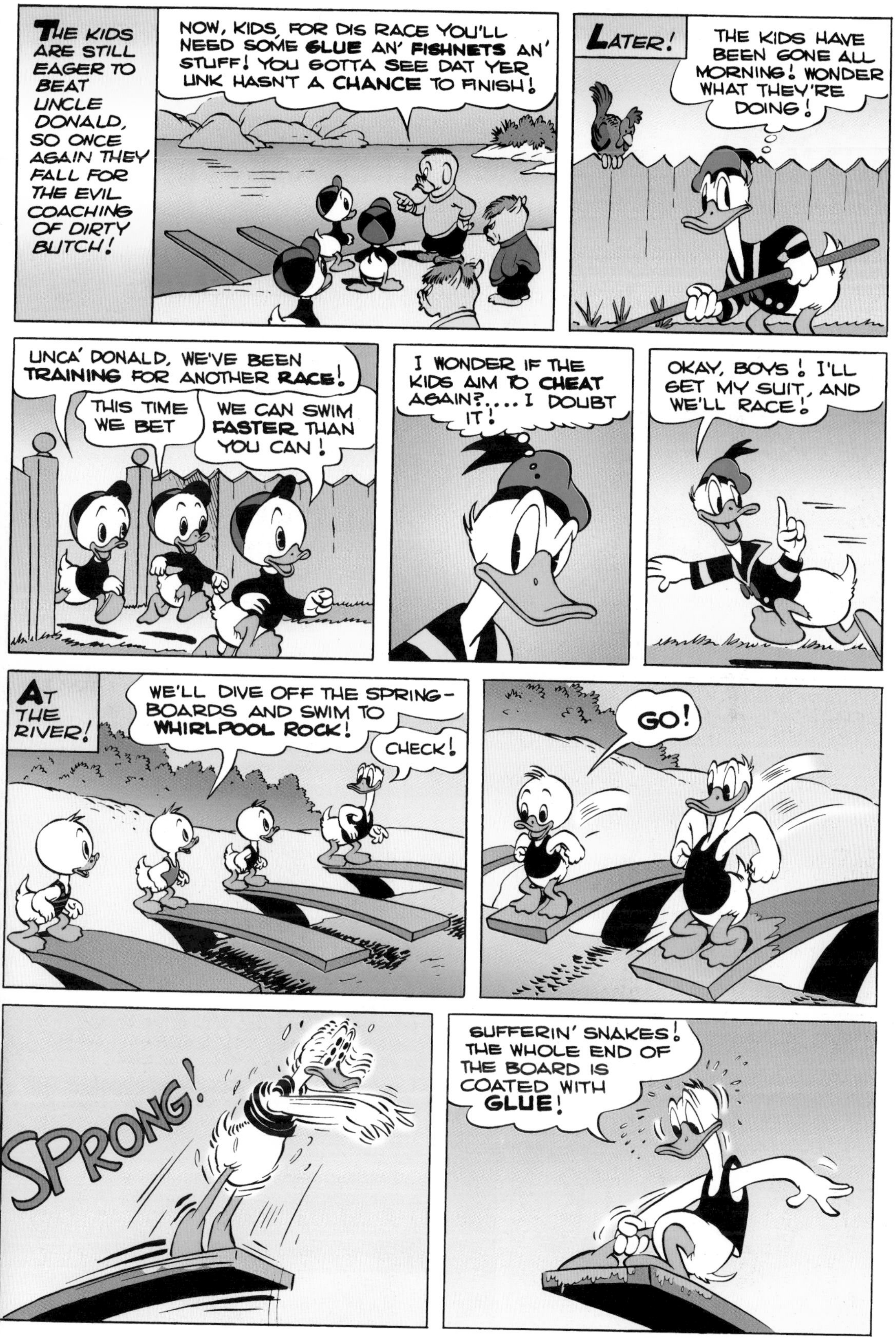
THE KIDS ARE STILL EAGER TO BEAT UNCLE DONALD, SO ONCE AGAIN THEY FALL FOR THE EVIL COACHING OF DIRTY BUTCH!
NOW, KIDS, FOR DIS RACE YOU'LL NEED SOME GLUE AN' FISHNETS AN' STUFF! YOU GOTTA SEE DAT YER UNK HASN'T A CHANCE TO FINISH!
LATER!
THE KIDS HAVE BEEN GONE ALL MORNING! WONDER WHAT THEY'RE DOING!
UNCA' DONALD, WE'VE BEEN TRAINING FOR ANOTHER RACE!
THIS TIME WE BET
WE CAN SWIM FASTER THAN YOU CAN!
I WONDER IF THE KIDS AIM TO CHEAT AGAIN?.... I DOUBT IT!
OKAY, BOYS! I'LL GET MY SUIT, AND WE'LL RACE!
AT THE RIVER!
WE'LL DIVE OFF THE SPRING-BOARDS AND SWIM TO WHIRLPOOL ROCK!
CHECK!
GO!
SPRONG!
SUFFERIN' SNAKES! THE WHOLE END OF THE BOARD IS COATED WITH GLUE!

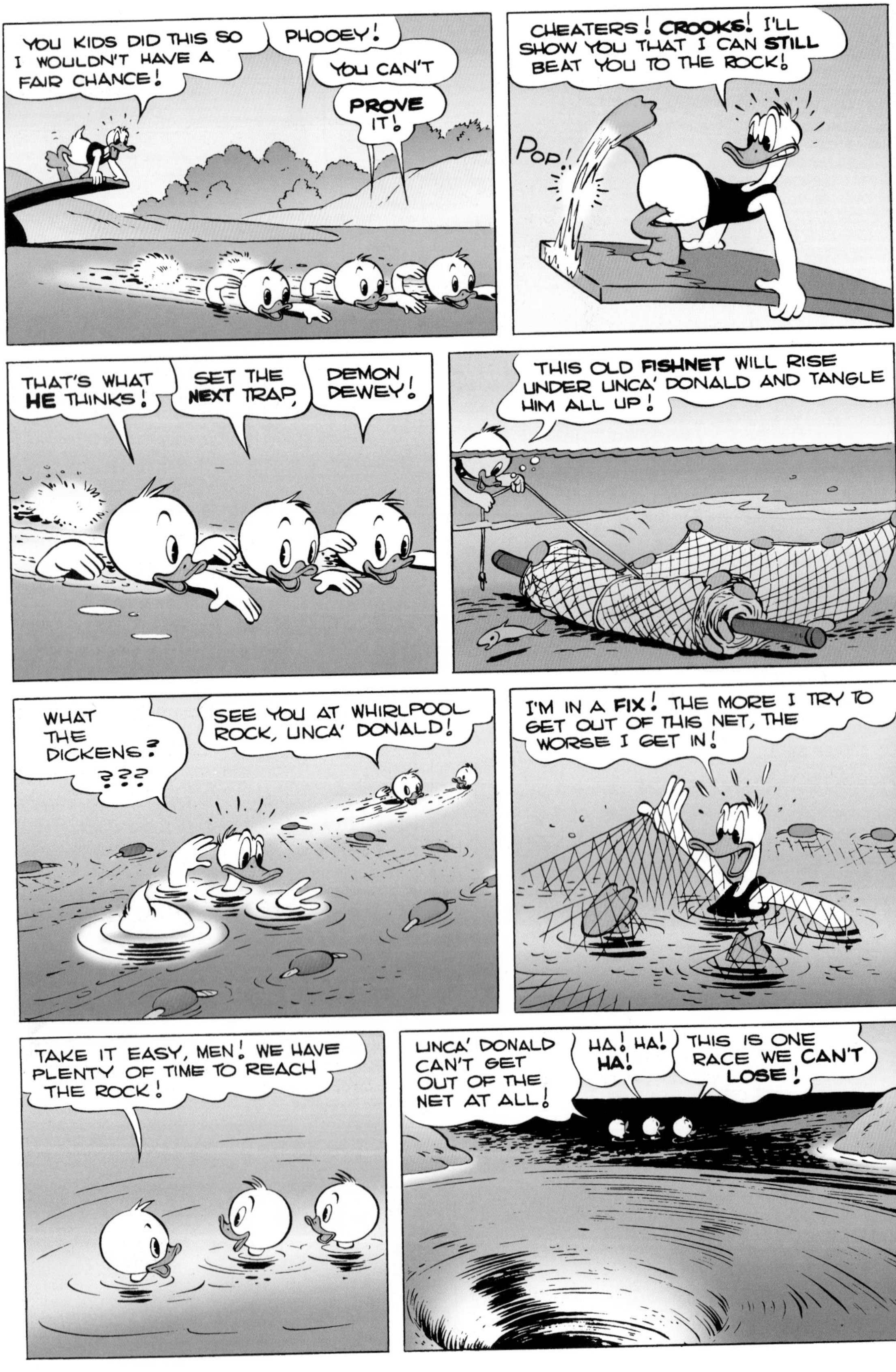

YOU KIDS DID THIS SO I WOULDN'T HAVE A FAIR CHANCE!
PHOOEY!
YOU CAN'T
PROVE IT!
CHEATERS! CROOKS! I'LL SHOW YOU THAT I CAN STILL BEAT YOU TO THE ROCK!
POP!
THAT'S WHAT HE THINKS!
SET THE NEXT TRAP,
DEMON DEWEY!
THIS OLD FISHNET WILL RISE UNDER UNCA' DONALD AND TANGLE HIM ALL UP!
WHAT THE DICKENS? ???
SEE YOU AT WHIRLPOOL ROCK, UNCA' DONALD!
I'M IN A FIX! THE MORE I TRY TO GET OUT OF THIS NET, THE WORSE I GET IN!
TAKE IT EASY, MEN! WE HAVE PLENTY OF TIME TO REACH THE ROCK!
UNCA' DONALD CAN'T GET OUT OF THE NET AT ALL!
HA! HA! HA!
THIS IS ONE RACE WE CAN'T LOSE!

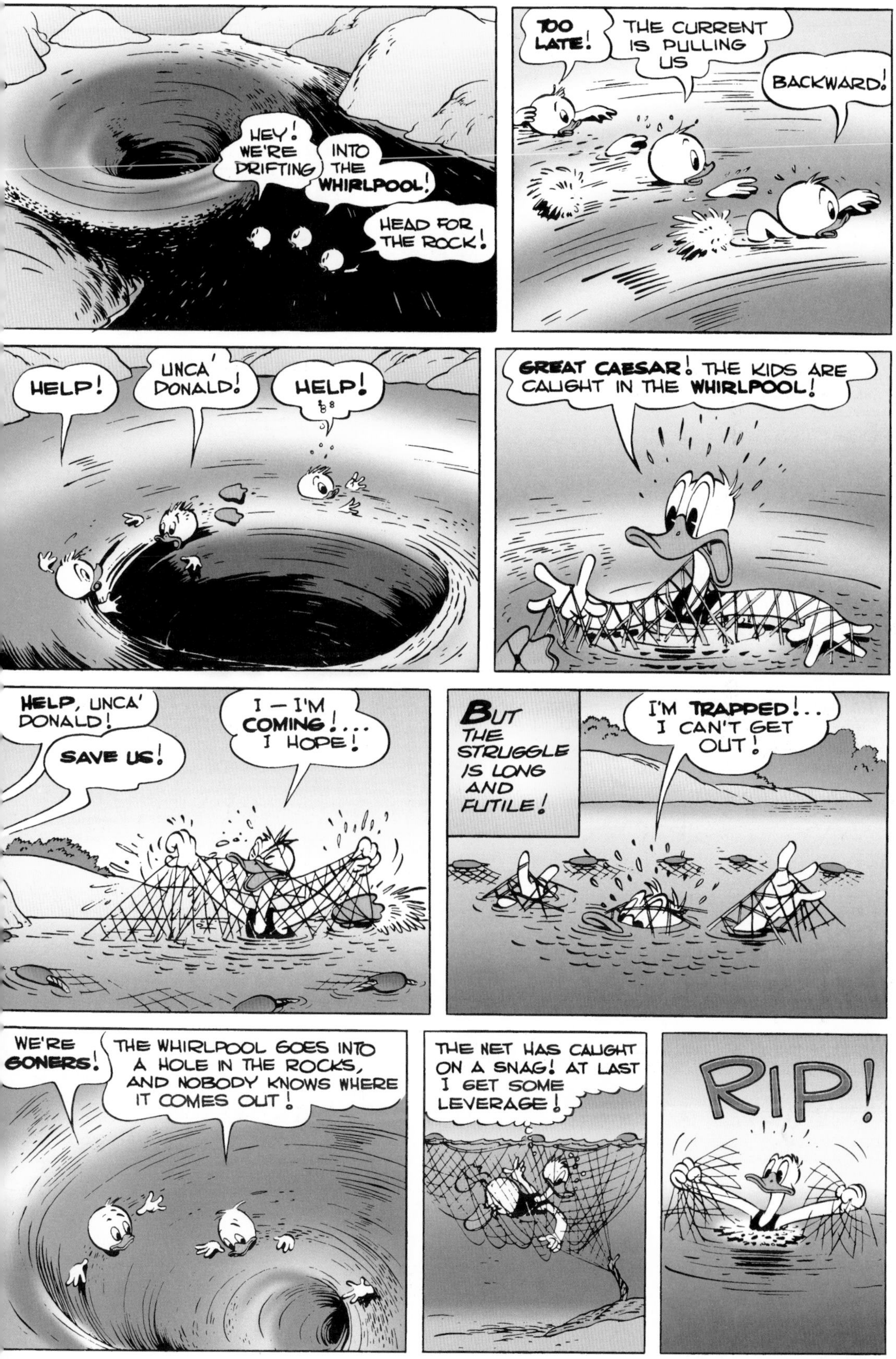

HEY! WE'RE DRIFTING
INTO THE WHIRLPOOL!
HEAD FOR THE ROCK!
TOO LATE!
THE CURRENT IS PULLING US
BACKWARD!
HELP!
UNCA' DONALD!
HELP!
GREAT CAESAR! THE KIDS ARE CAUGHT IN THE WHIRLPOOL!
HELP, UNCA' DONALD!
SAVE US!
I — I'M COMING!... I HOPE!
BUT THE STRUGGLE IS LONG AND FUTILE!
I'M TRAPPED!.. I CAN'T GET OUT!
WE'RE GONERS!
THE WHIRLPOOL GOES INTO A HOLE IN THE ROCKS, AND NOBODY KNOWS WHERE IT COMES OUT!
THE NET HAS CAUGHT ON A SNAG! AT LAST I GET SOME LEVERAGE!
RIP!

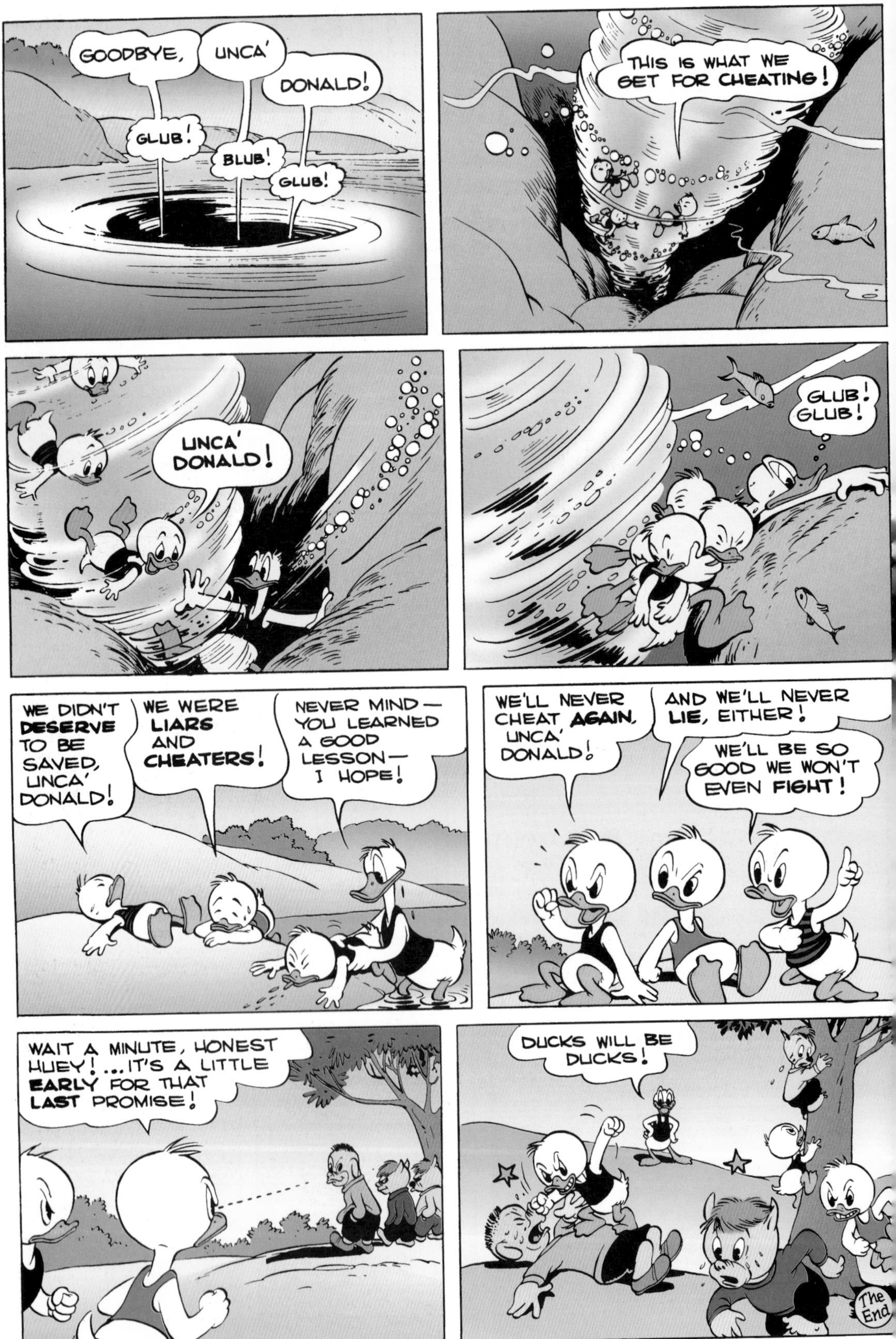
GOODBYE,
UNCA'
DONALD!
GLUB!
BLUB!
GLUB!
THIS IS WHAT WE GET FOR CHEATING!
UNCA' DONALD!
GLUB! GLUB!
WE DIDN'T DESERVE TO BE SAVED, UNCA' DONALD!
WE WERE LIARS AND CHEATERS!
NEVER MIND— YOU LEARNED A GOOD LESSON— I HOPE!
WE'LL NEVER CHEAT AGAIN, UNCA' DONALD!
AND WE'LL NEVER LIE, EITHER!
WE'LL BE SO GOOD WE WON'T EVEN FIGHT!
WAIT A MINUTE, HONEST HUEY! ...IT'S A LITTLE EARLY FOR THAT LAST PROMISE!
DUCKS WILL BE DUCKS!
The End

Walt Disney's Mickey Mouse in

MUMMY DEAREST

PART ONE

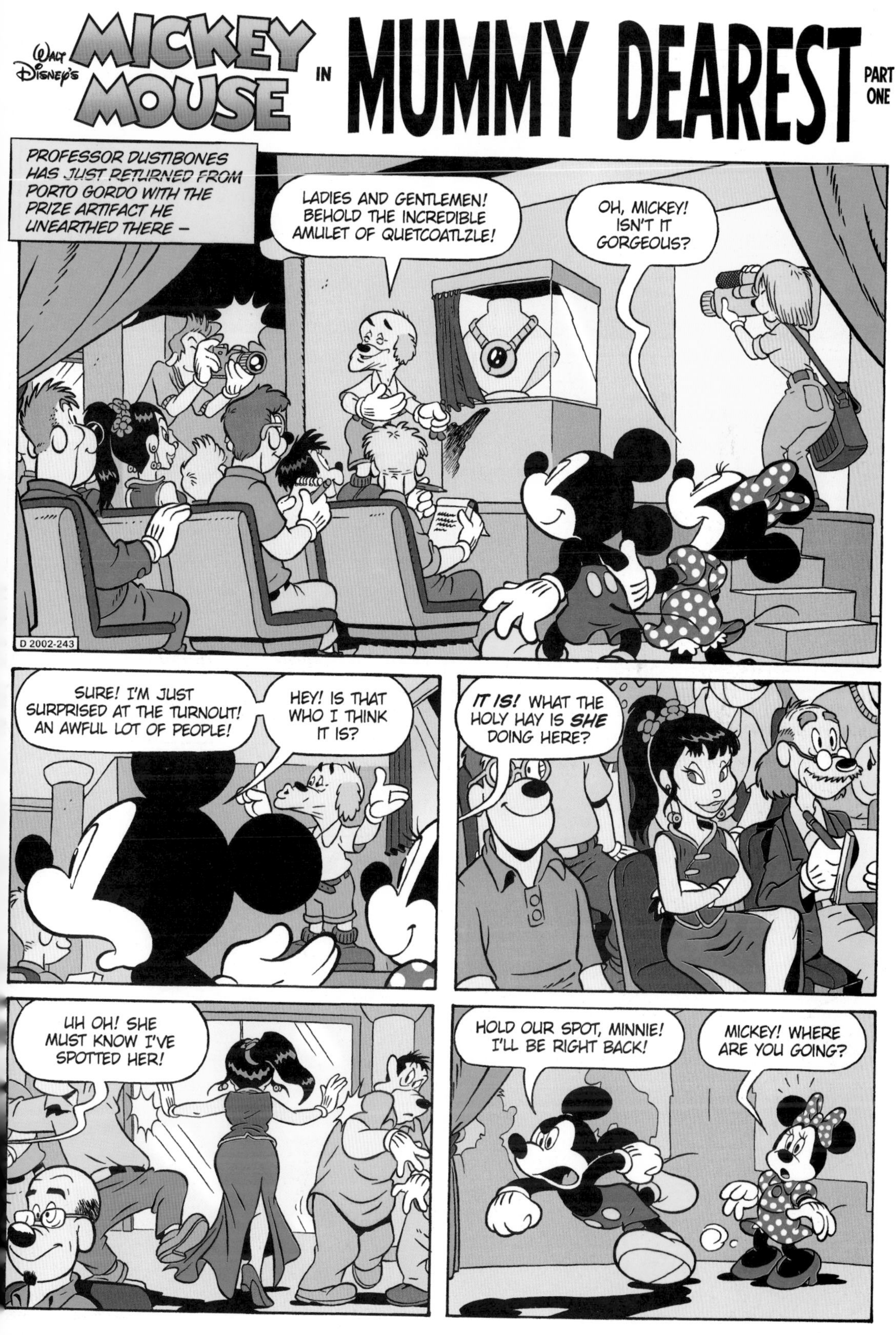
PROFESSOR DUSTIBONES HAS JUST RETURNED FROM PORTO GORDO WITH THE PRIZE ARTIFACT HE UNEARTHED THERE –
LADIES AND GENTLEMEN! BEHOLD THE INCREDIBLE AMULET OF QUETCOATLZLE!
OH, MICKEY! ISN'T IT GORGEOUS?
D 2002-243
SURE! I'M JUST SURPRISED AT THE TURNOUT! AN AWFUL LOT OF PEOPLE!
HEY! IS THAT WHO I THINK IT IS?
IT IS! WHAT THE HOLY HAY IS SHE DOING HERE?
UH OH! SHE MUST KNOW I'VE SPOTTED HER!
HOLD OUR SPOT, MINNIE! I'LL BE RIGHT BACK!
MICKEY! WHERE ARE YOU GOING?

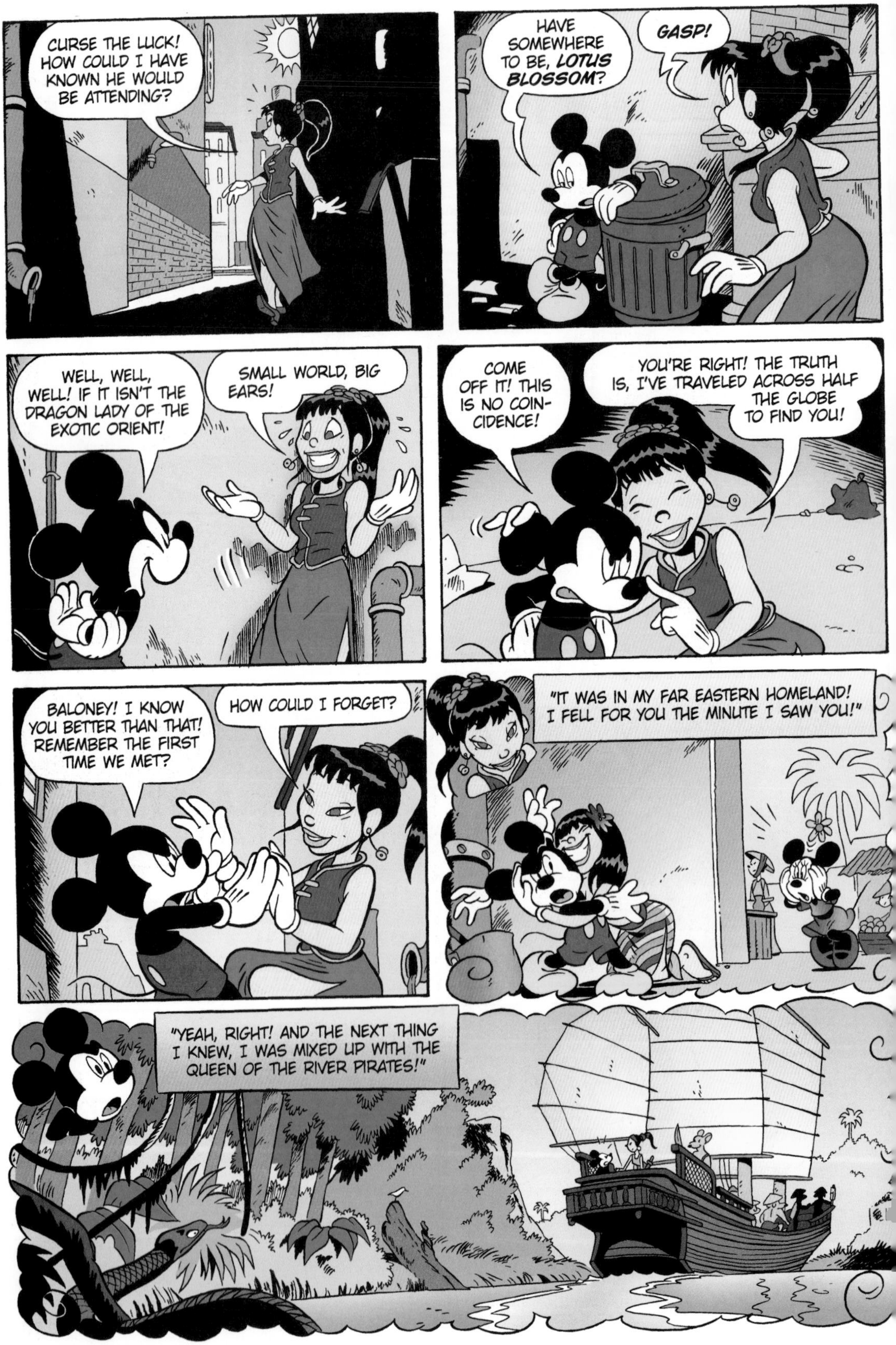
CURSE THE LUCK! HOW COULD I HAVE KNOWN HE WOULD BE ATTENDING?
HAVE SOMEWHERE TO BE, LOTUS BLOSSOM?
GASP!
WELL, WELL, WELL! IF IT ISN'T THE DRAGON LADY OF THE EXOTIC ORIENT!
SMALL WORLD, BIG EARS!
COME OFF IT! THIS IS NO COIN- CIDENCE!
YOU'RE RIGHT! THE TRUTH IS, I'VE TRAVELED ACROSS HALF THE GLOBE TO FIND YOU!
BALONEY! I KNOW YOU BETTER THAN THAT! REMEMBER THE FIRST TIME WE MET?
HOW COULD I FORGET?
"IT WAS IN MY FAR EASTERN HOMELAND! I FELL FOR YOU THE MINUTE I SAW YOU!"
"YEAH, RIGHT! AND THE NEXT THING I KNEW, I WAS MIXED UP WITH THE QUEEN OF THE RIVER PIRATES!"

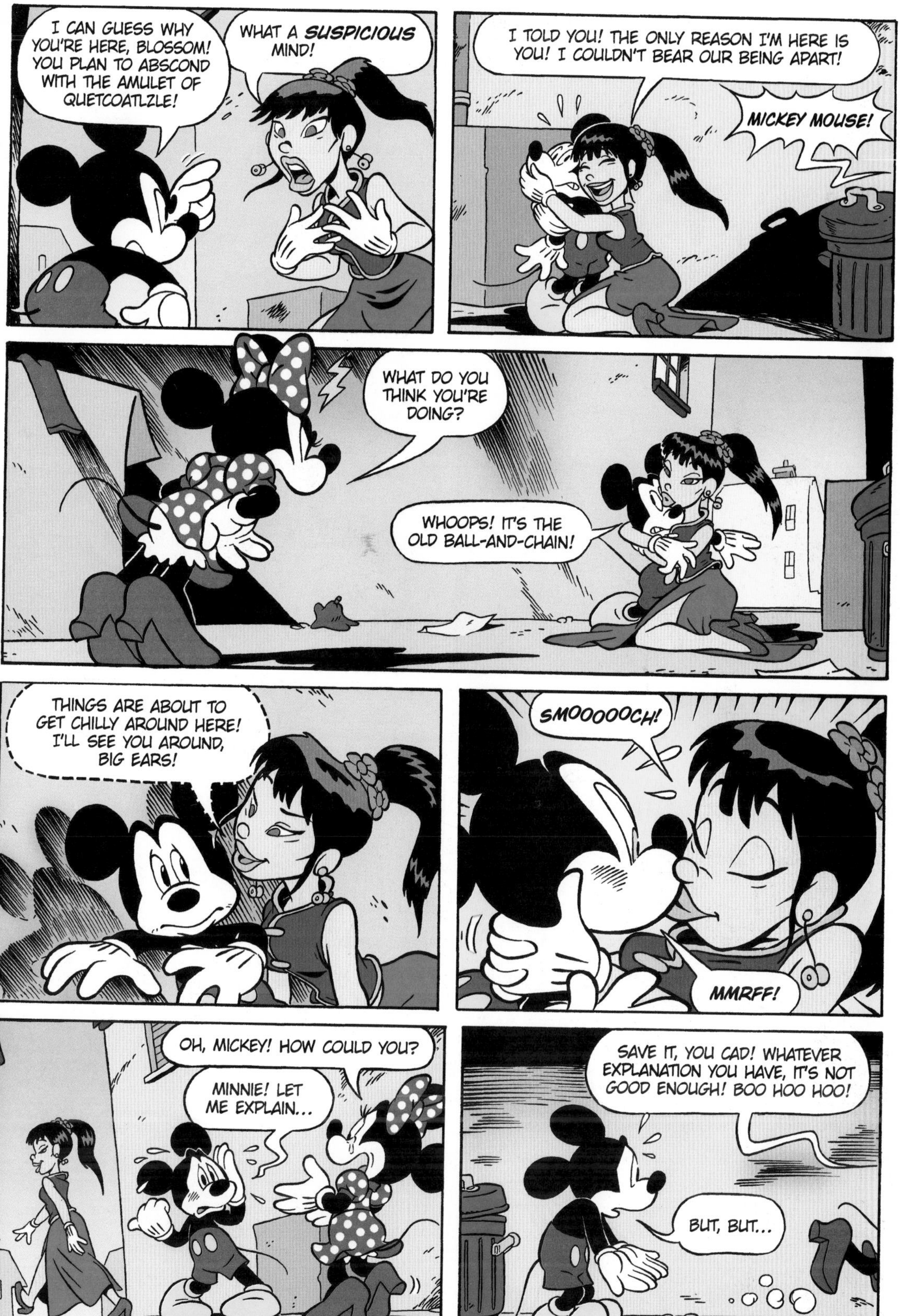
I CAN GUESS WHY YOU'RE HERE, BLOSSOM! YOU PLAN TO ABSCOND WITH THE AMULET OF QUETCOATLZLE!
WHAT A SUSPICIOUS MIND!
I TOLD YOU! THE ONLY REASON I'M HERE IS YOU! I COULDN'T BEAR OUR BEING APART!
MICKEY MOUSE!
WHAT DO YOU THINK YOU'RE DOING?
WHOOPS! IT'S THE OLD BALL-AND-CHAIN!
THINGS ARE ABOUT TO GET CHILLY AROUND HERE! I'LL SEE YOU AROUND, BIG EARS!
SMOOOOOCH!
MMRFF!
OH, MICKEY! HOW COULD YOU?
MINNIE! LET ME EXPLAIN...
SAVE IT, YOU CAD! WHATEVER EXPLANATION YOU HAVE, IT'S NOT GOOD ENOUGH! BOO HOO HOO!
BUT, BUT...

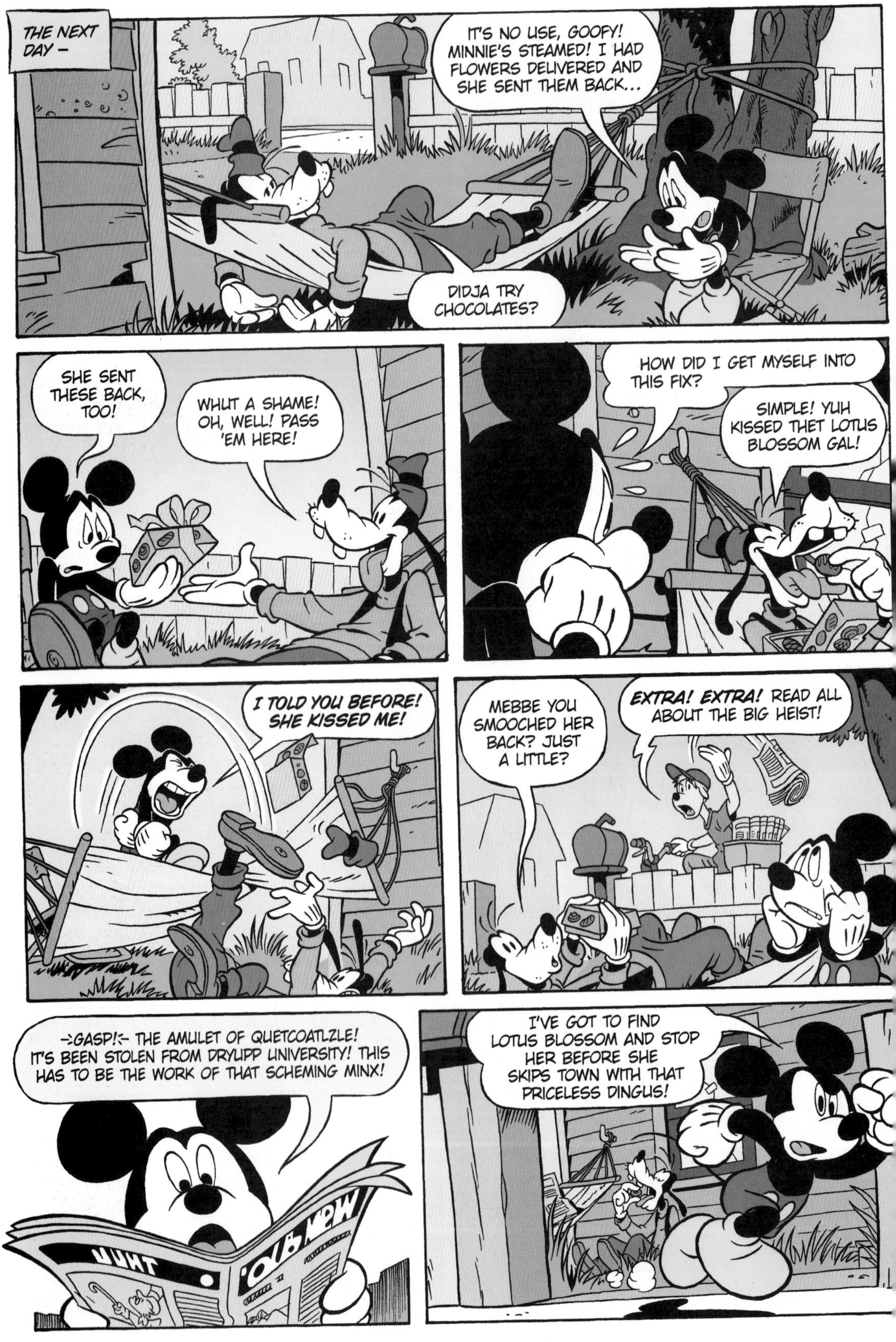
THE NEXT DAY –
IT'S NO USE, GOOFY! MINNIE'S STEAMED! I HAD FLOWERS DELIVERED AND SHE SENT THEM BACK...
DIDJA TRY CHOCOLATES?
SHE SENT THESE BACK, TOO!
WHUT A SHAME! OH, WELL! PASS 'EM HERE!
HOW DID I GET MYSELF INTO THIS FIX?
SIMPLE! YUH KISSED THET LOTUS BLOSSOM GAL!
I TOLD YOU BEFORE! SHE KISSED ME!
MEBBE YOU SMOOCHED HER BACK? JUST A LITTLE?
EXTRA! EXTRA! READ ALL ABOUT THE BIG HEIST!
–GASP!– THE AMULET OF QUETCOATLZLE! IT'S BEEN STOLEN FROM DRYUPP UNIVERSITY! THIS HAS TO BE THE WORK OF THAT SCHEMING MINX!
I'VE GOT TO FIND LOTUS BLOSSOM AND STOP HER BEFORE SHE SKIPS TOWN WITH THAT PRICELESS DINGUS!

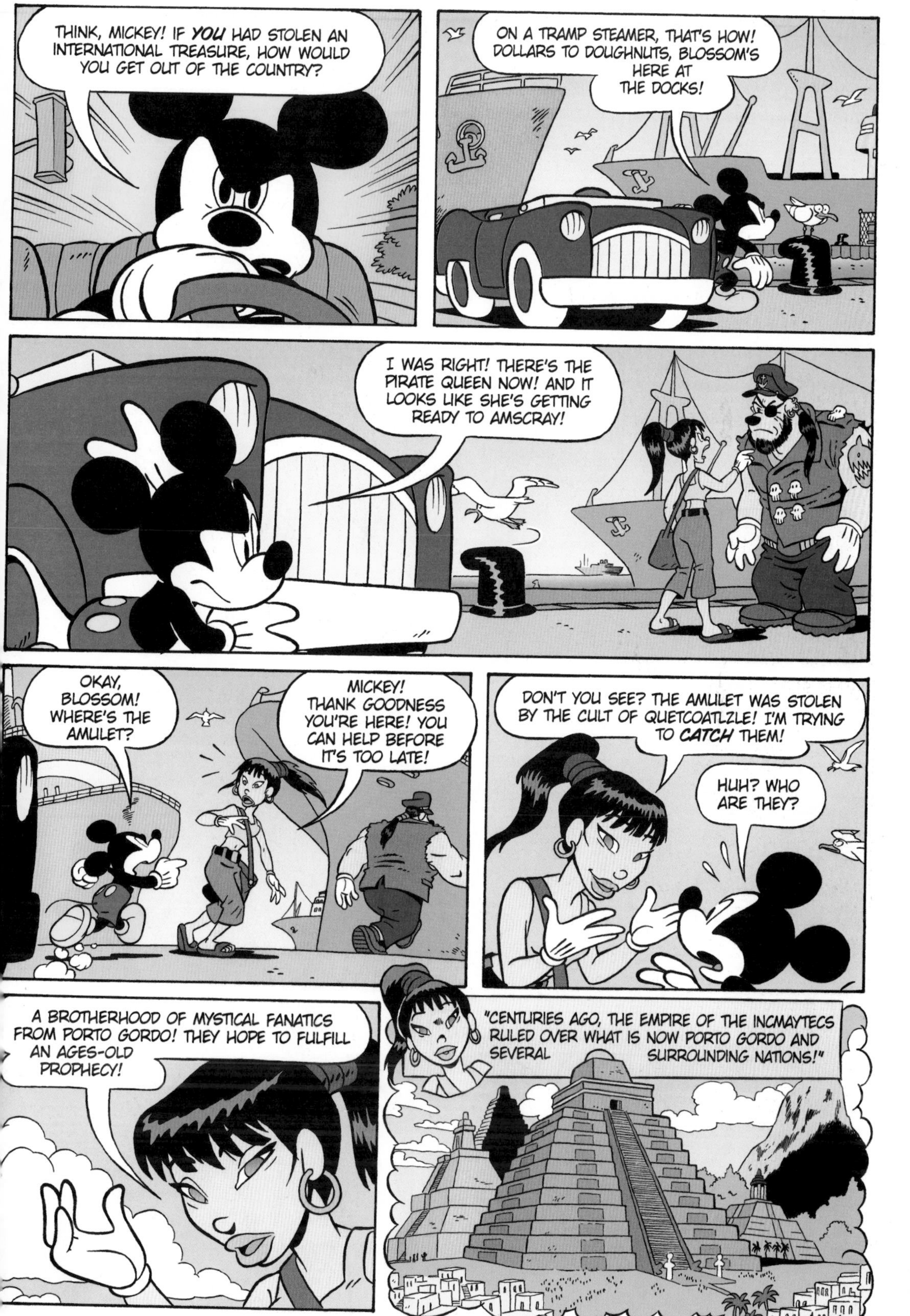

THINK, MICKEY! IF *YOU* HAD STOLEN AN INTERNATIONAL TREASURE, HOW WOULD YOU GET OUT OF THE COUNTRY?
ON A TRAMP STEAMER, THAT'S HOW! DOLLARS TO DOUGHNUTS, BLOSSOM'S HERE AT THE DOCKS!
I WAS RIGHT! THERE'S THE PIRATE QUEEN NOW! AND IT LOOKS LIKE SHE'S GETTING READY TO AMSCRAY!
OKAY, BLOSSOM! WHERE'S THE AMULET?
MICKEY! THANK GOODNESS YOU'RE HERE! YOU CAN HELP BEFORE IT'S TOO LATE!
DON'T YOU SEE? THE AMULET WAS STOLEN BY THE CULT OF QUETCOATLZLE! I'M TRYING TO *CATCH* THEM!
HUH? WHO ARE THEY?
A BROTHERHOOD OF MYSTICAL FANATICS FROM PORTO GORDO! THEY HOPE TO FULFILL AN AGES-OLD PROPHECY!
"CENTURIES AGO, THE EMPIRE OF THE INCMAYTECS RULED OVER WHAT IS NOW PORTO GORDO AND SEVERAL SURROUNDING NATIONS!"

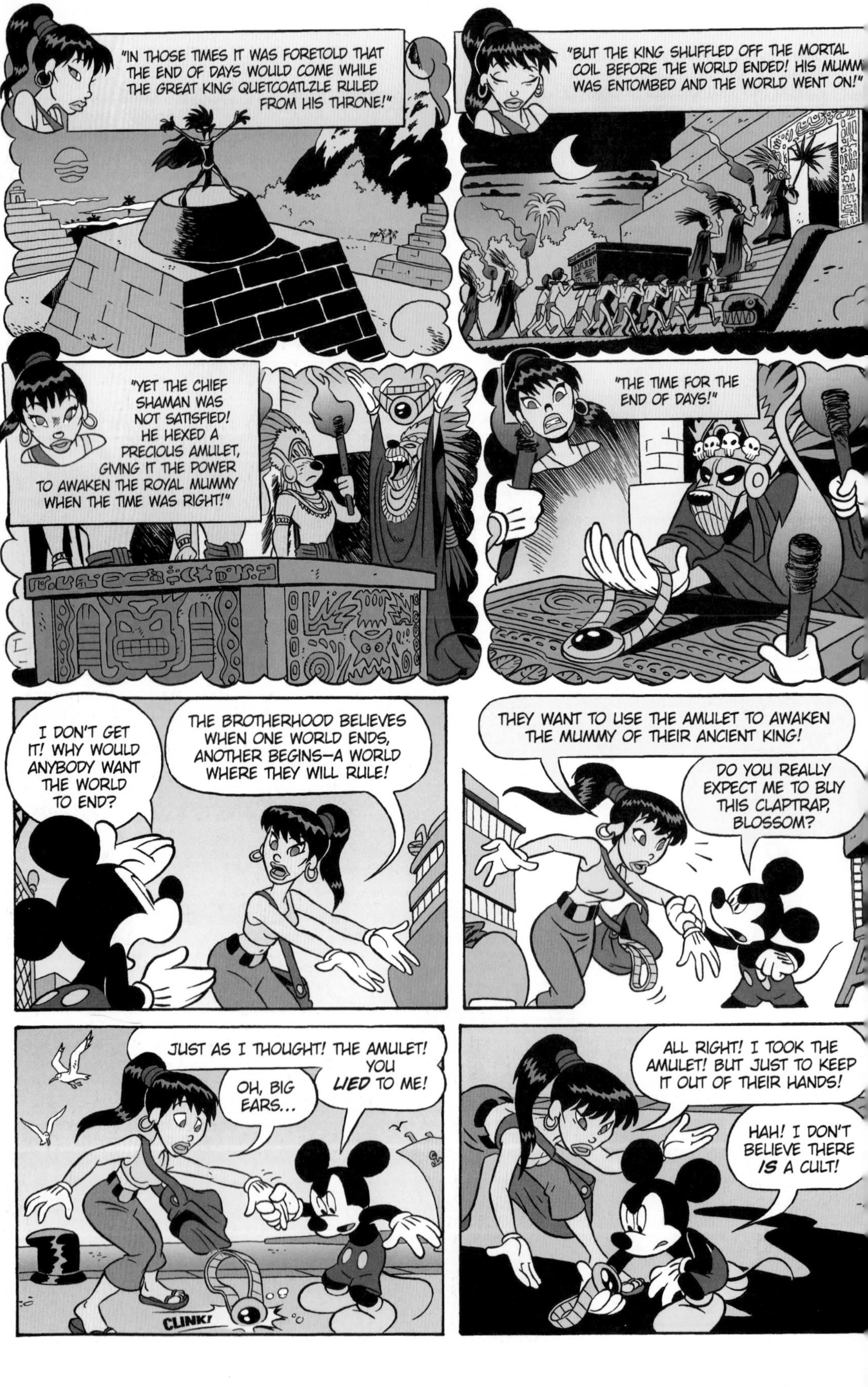
"IN THOSE TIMES IT WAS FORETOLD THAT THE END OF DAYS WOULD COME WHILE THE GREAT KING QUETCOATLZLE RULED FROM HIS THRONE!"
"BUT THE KING SHUFFLED OFF THE MORTAL COIL BEFORE THE WORLD ENDED! HIS MUMM WAS ENTOMBED AND THE WORLD WENT ON!"
"YET THE CHIEF SHAMAN WAS NOT SATISFIED! HE HEXED A PRECIOUS AMULET, GIVING IT THE POWER TO AWAKEN THE ROYAL MUMMY WHEN THE TIME WAS RIGHT!"
"THE TIME FOR THE END OF DAYS!"
I DON'T GET IT! WHY WOULD ANYBODY WANT THE WORLD TO END?
THE BROTHERHOOD BELIEVES WHEN ONE WORLD ENDS, ANOTHER BEGINS—A WORLD WHERE THEY WILL RULE!
THEY WANT TO USE THE AMULET TO AWAKEN THE MUMMY OF THEIR ANCIENT KING!
DO YOU REALLY EXPECT ME TO BUY THIS CLAPTRAP, BLOSSOM?
JUST AS I THOUGHT! THE AMULET! YOU LIED TO ME!
OH, BIG EARS...
CLINK!
ALL RIGHT! I TOOK THE AMULET! BUT JUST TO KEEP IT OUT OF THEIR HANDS!
HAH! I DON'T BELIEVE THERE IS A CULT!

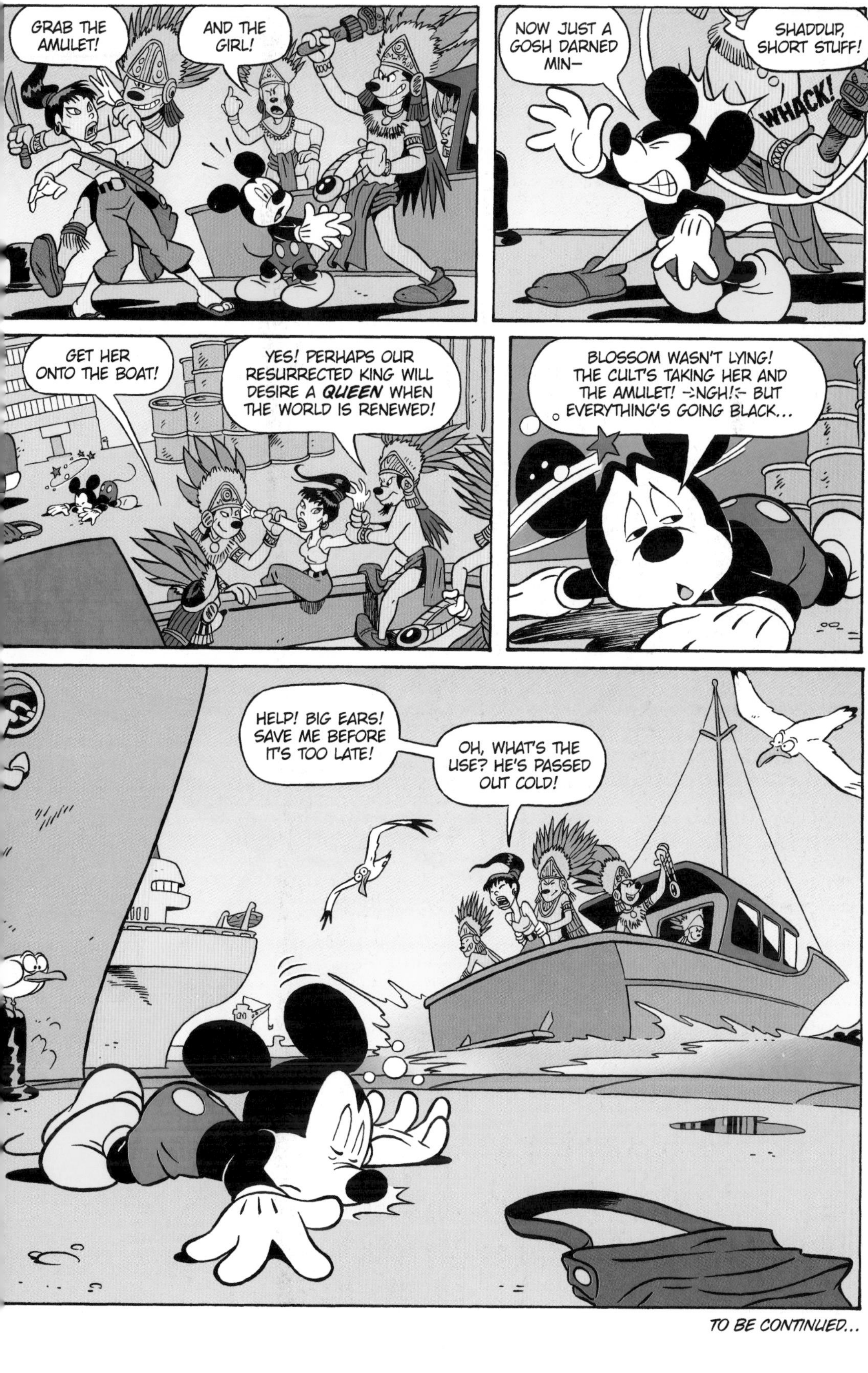
GRAB THE AMULET!
AND THE GIRL!
NOW JUST A GOSH DARNED MIN—
SHADDUP, SHORT STUFF!
WHACK!
GET HER ONTO THE BOAT!
YES! PERHAPS OUR RESURRECTED KING WILL DESIRE A ***QUEEN*** WHEN THE WORLD IS RENEWED!
BLOSSOM WASN'T LYING! THE CULT'S TAKING HER AND THE AMULET! –NGH!– BUT EVERYTHING'S GOING BLACK...
HELP! BIG EARS! SAVE ME BEFORE IT'S TOO LATE!
OH, WHAT'S THE USE? HE'S PASSED OUT COLD!

TO BE CONTINUED...

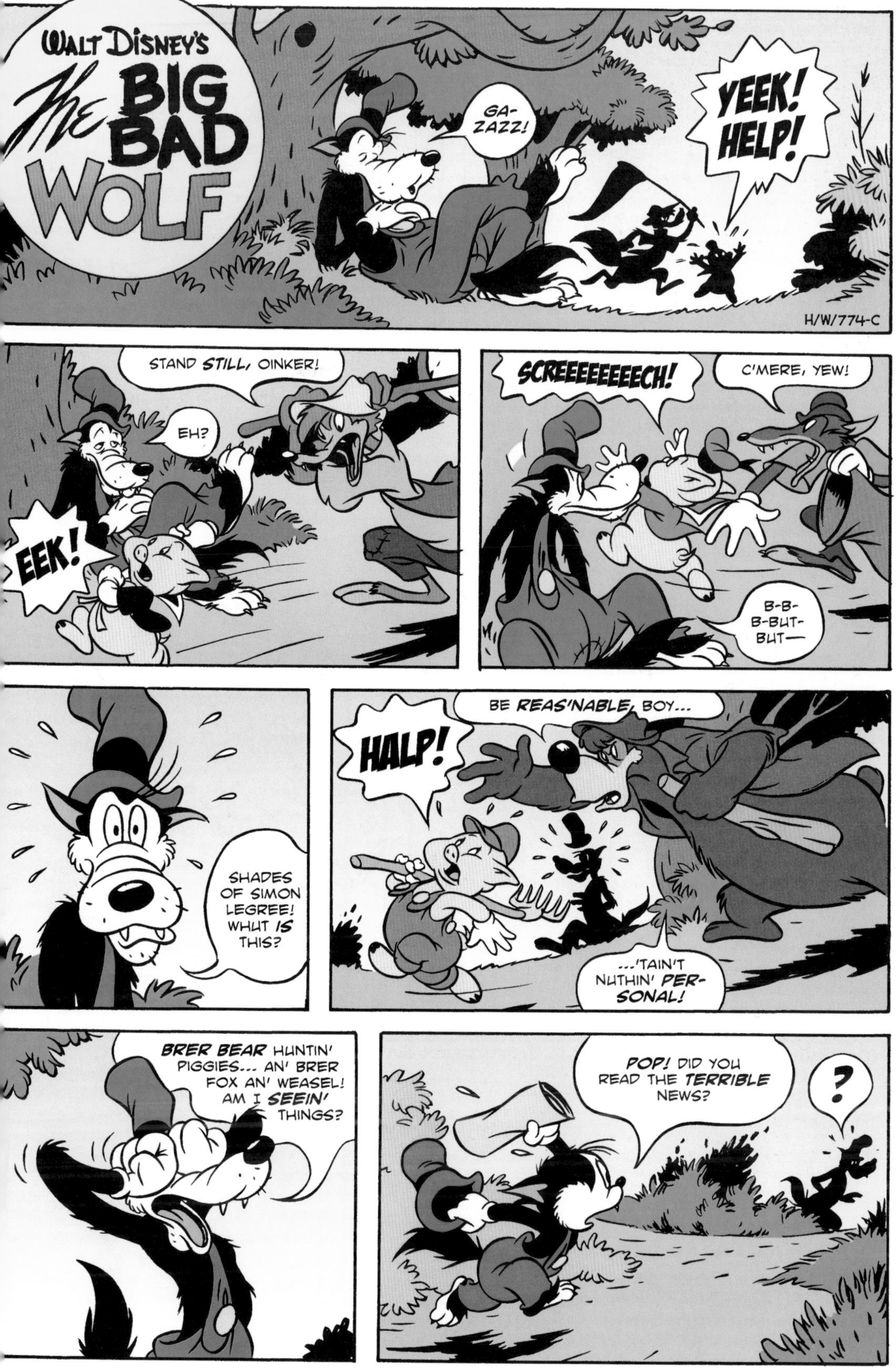
WALT DISNEY'S
THE BIG BAD WOLF
GA-ZAZZ!
YEEK! HELP!
H/W/774-C
STAND STILL, OINKER!
EH?
EEK!
SCREEEEEEEECH!
C'MERE, YEW!
B-B-B-BUT-BUT—
SHADES OF SIMON LEGREE! WHUT IS THIS?
BE REAS'NABLE, BOY...
HALP!
...'TAIN'T NUTHIN' PERSONAL!
BRER BEAR HUNTIN' PIGGIES... AN' BRER FOX AN' WEASEL! AM I SEEIN' THINGS?
POP! DID YOU READ THE TERRIBLE NEWS?
?

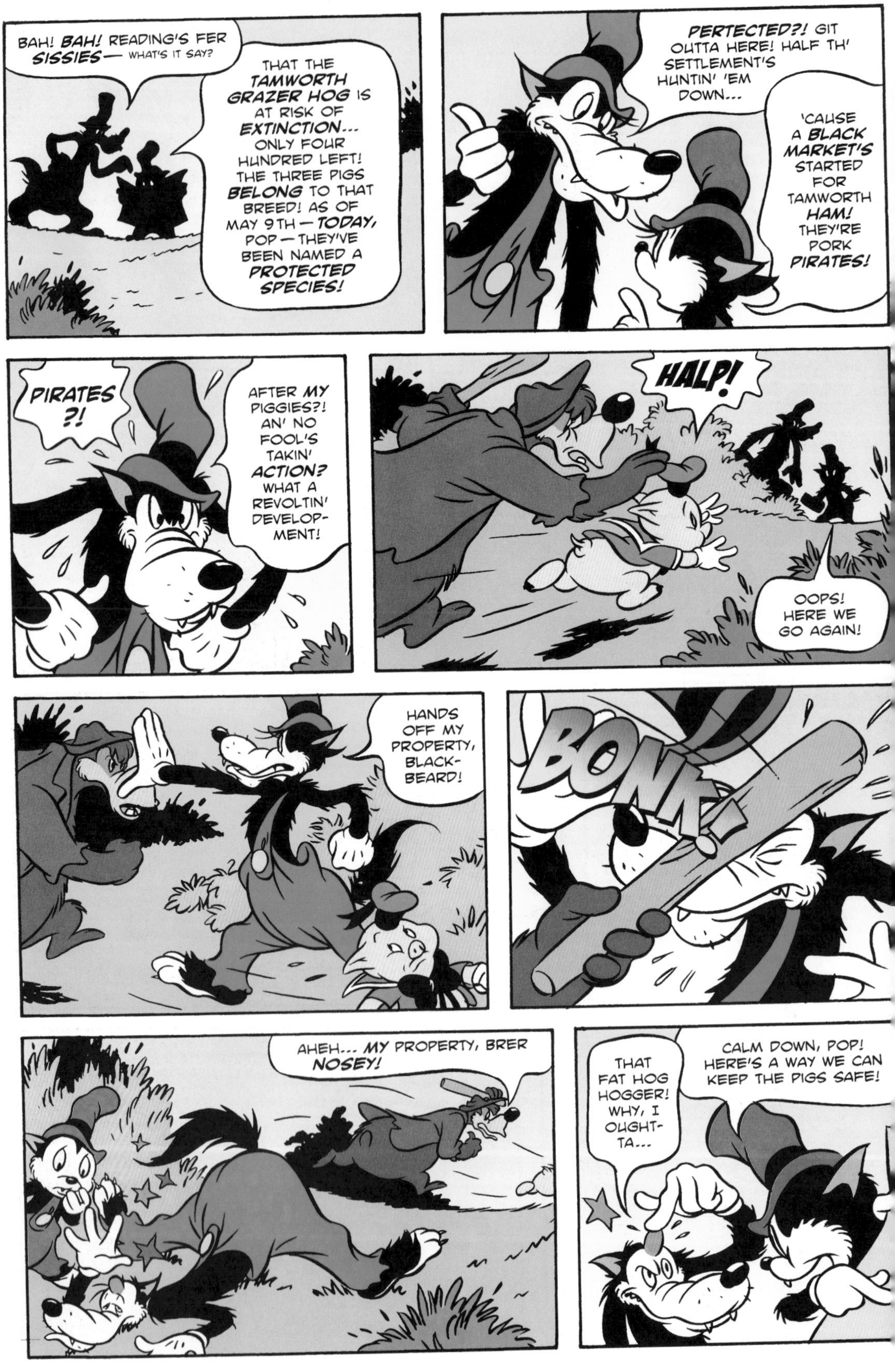
BAH! BAH! READING'S FER SISSIES— WHAT'S IT SAY?
THAT THE TAMWORTH GRAZER HOG IS AT RISK OF EXTINCTION... ONLY FOUR HUNDRED LEFT! THE THREE PIGS BELONG TO THAT BREED! AS OF MAY 9TH—TODAY, POP—THEY'VE BEEN NAMED A PROTECTED SPECIES!
PERTECTED?! GIT OUTTA HERE! HALF TH' SETTLEMENT'S HUNTIN' 'EM DOWN...
'CAUSE A BLACK MARKET'S STARTED FOR TAMWORTH HAM! THEY'RE PORK PIRATES!
PIRATES ?!
AFTER MY PIGGIES?! AN' NO FOOL'S TAKIN' ACTION? WHAT A REVOLTIN' DEVELOP-MENT!
HALP!
OOPS! HERE WE GO AGAIN!
HANDS OFF MY PROPERTY, BLACK-BEARD!
BONK!
AHEH... MY PROPERTY, BRER NOSEY!
THAT FAT HOG HOGGER! WHY, I OUGHT-TA...
CALM DOWN, POP! HERE'S A WAY WE CAN KEEP THE PIGS SAFE!

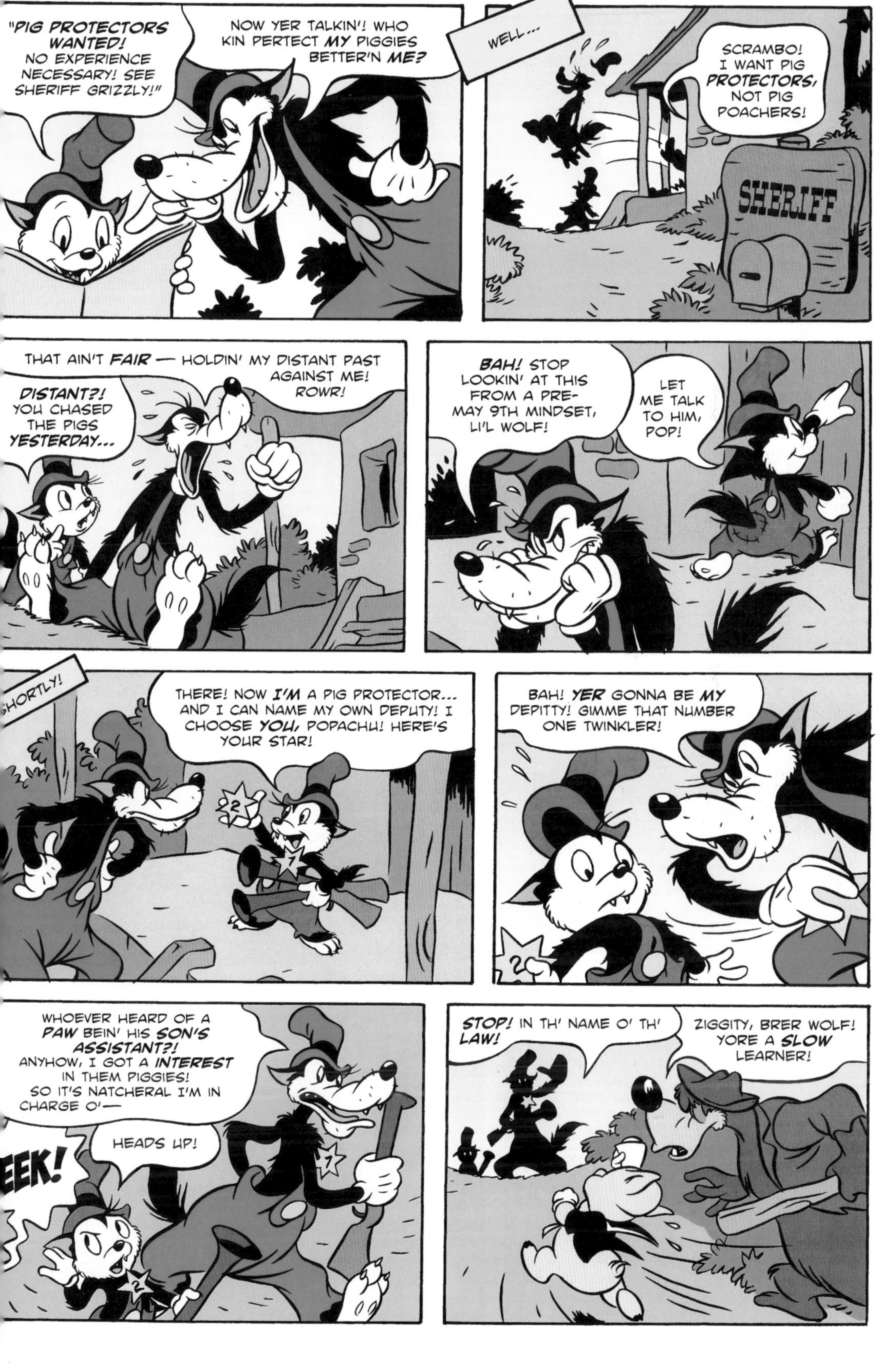
"PIG PROTECTORS WANTED! NO EXPERIENCE NECESSARY! SEE SHERIFF GRIZZLY!"
NOW YER TALKIN'! WHO KIN PERTECT MY PIGGIES BETTER'N ME?
WELL...
SCRAMBO! I WANT PIG PROTECTORS, NOT PIG POACHERS!
SHERIFF
THAT AIN'T FAIR — HOLDIN' MY DISTANT PAST AGAINST ME! ROWR!
DISTANT?! YOU CHASED THE PIGS YESTERDAY...
BAH! STOP LOOKIN' AT THIS FROM A PRE-MAY 9TH MINDSET, LI'L WOLF!
LET ME TALK TO HIM, POP!
SHORTLY!
THERE! NOW I'M A PIG PROTECTOR... AND I CAN NAME MY OWN DEPUTY! I CHOOSE YOU, POPACHU! HERE'S YOUR STAR!
BAH! YER GONNA BE MY DEPITTY! GIMME THAT NUMBER ONE TWINKLER!
WHOEVER HEARD OF A PAW BEIN' HIS SON'S ASSISTANT?! ANYHOW, I GOT A INTEREST IN THEM PIGGIES! SO IT'S NATCHERAL I'M IN CHARGE O'—
HEADS UP!
EEK!
STOP! IN TH' NAME O' TH' LAW!
ZIGGITY, BRER WOLF! YORE A SLOW LEARNER!

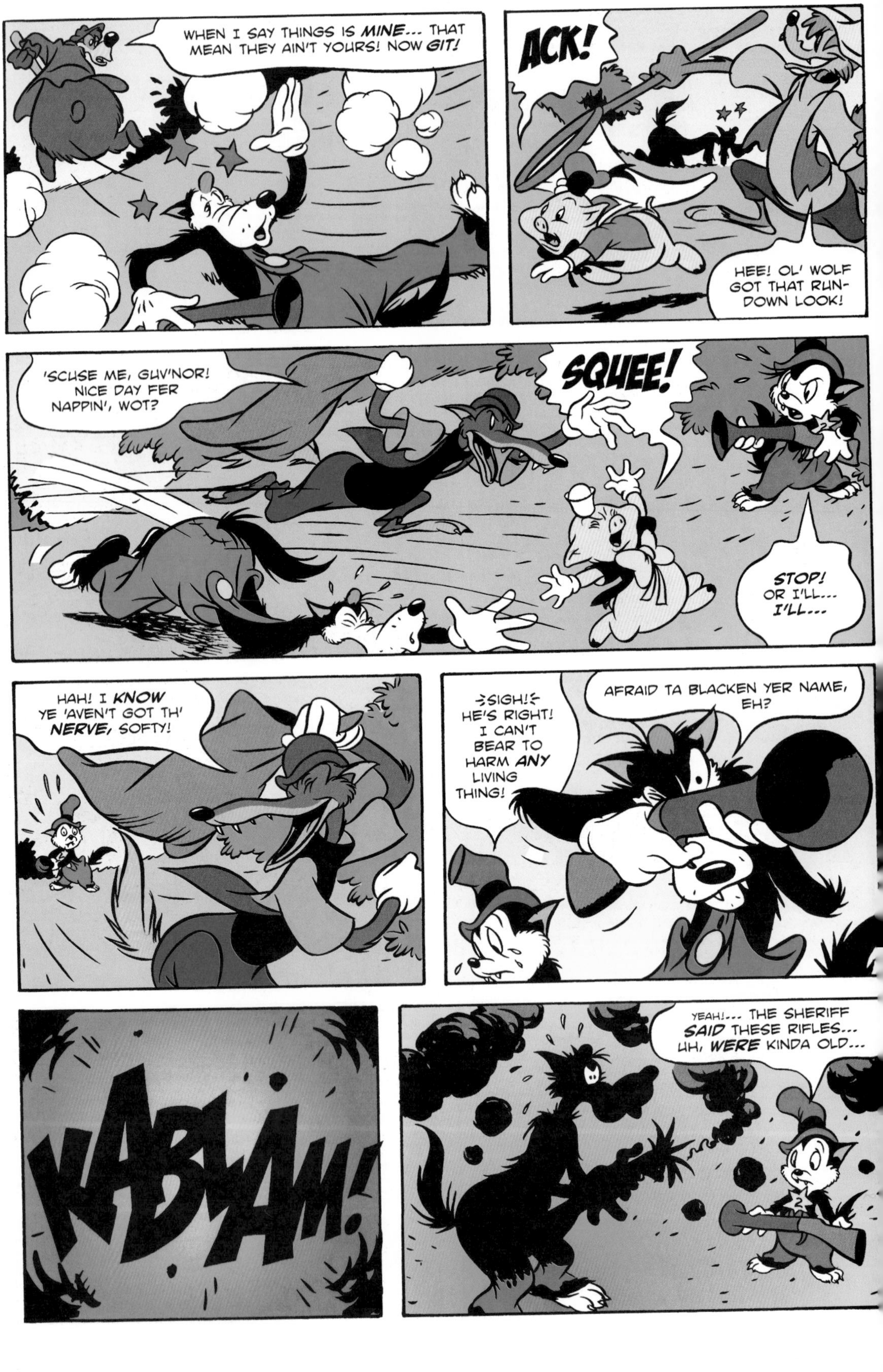
WHEN I SAY THINGS IS MINE... THAT MEAN THEY AIN'T YOURS! NOW GIT!
ACK!
HEE! OL' WOLF GOT THAT RUN-DOWN LOOK!
'SCUSE ME, GUV'NOR! NICE DAY FER NAPPIN', WOT?
SQUEE!
STOP! OR I'LL... I'LL...
HAH! I KNOW YE 'AVEN'T GOT TH' NERVE, SOFTY!
-SIGH!- HE'S RIGHT! I CAN'T BEAR TO HARM ANY LIVING THING!
AFRAID TA BLACKEN YER NAME, EH?
KABLAM!
YEAH!... THE SHERIFF SAID THESE RIFLES... UH, WERE KINDA OLD...

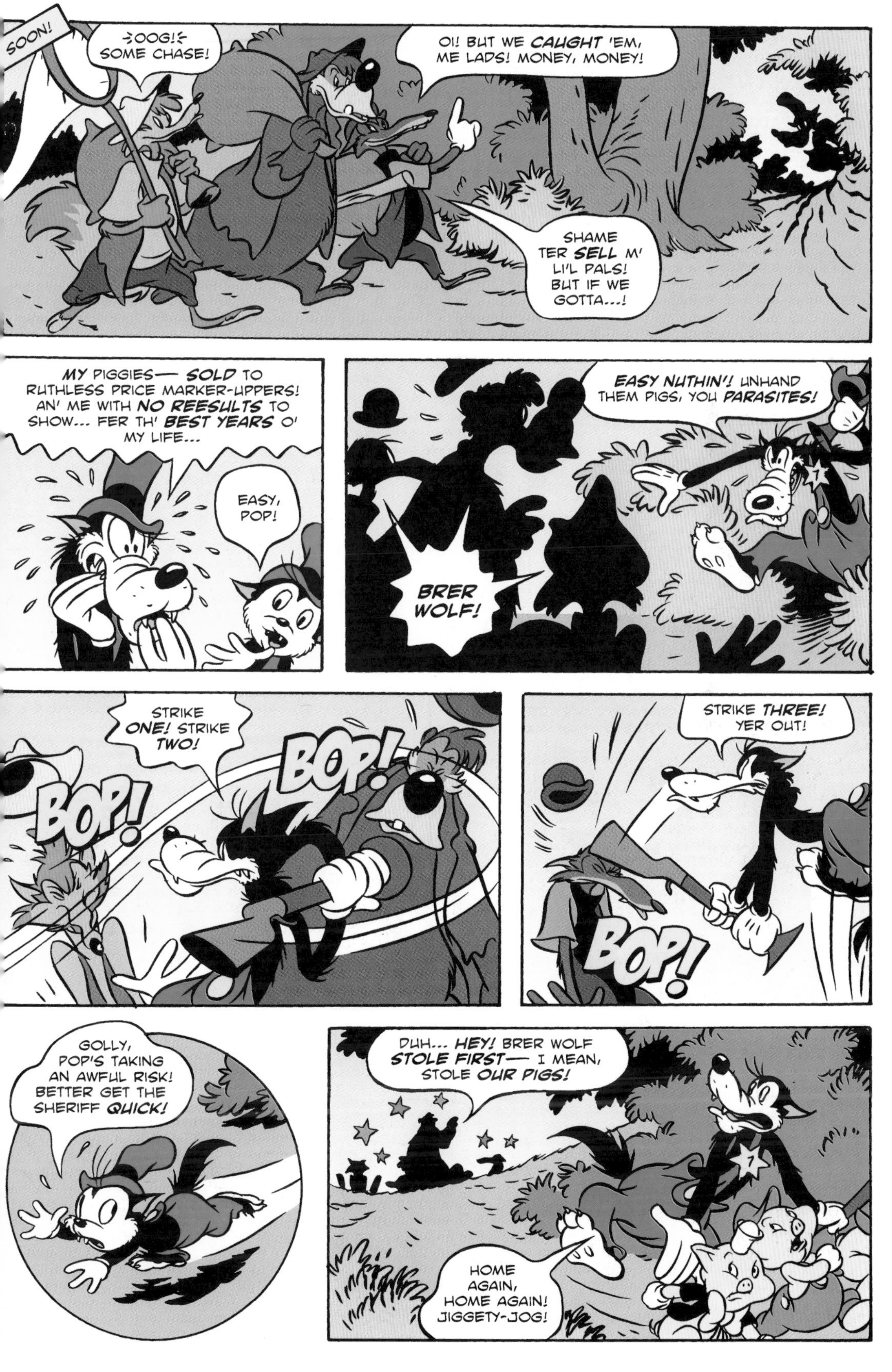
SOON!
≈OOG!≈
SOME CHASE!
OI! BUT WE CAUGHT 'EM, ME LADS! MONEY, MONEY!
SHAME TER SELL M' LI'L PALS! BUT IF WE GOTTA...!
MY PIGGIES— SOLD TO RUTHLESS PRICE MARKER-UPPERS! AN' ME WITH NO REESULTS TO SHOW... FER TH' BEST YEARS O' MY LIFE...
EASY, POP!
EASY NUTHIN'! UNHAND THEM PIGS, YOU PARASITES!
BRER WOLF!
STRIKE ONE! STRIKE TWO!
BOP!
BOP!
STRIKE THREE! YER OUT!
BOP!
GOLLY, POP'S TAKING AN AWFUL RISK! BETTER GET THE SHERIFF QUICK!
DUH... HEY! BRER WOLF STOLE FIRST— I MEAN, STOLE OUR PIGS!
HOME AGAIN, HOME AGAIN! JIGGETY-JOG!

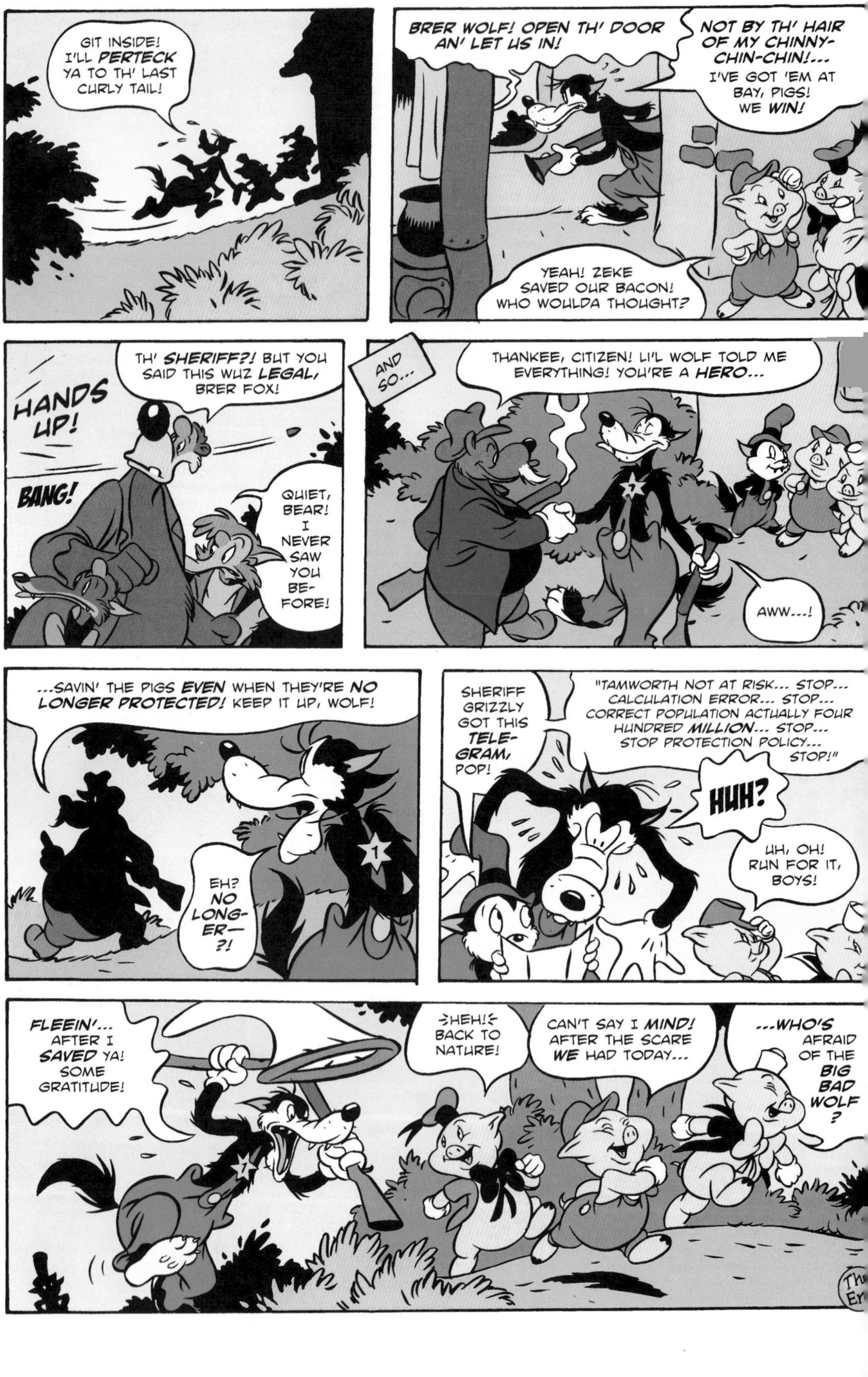
GIT INSIDE! I'LL PERTECK YA TO TH' LAST CURLY TAIL!
BRER WOLF! OPEN TH' DOOR AN' LET US IN!
NOT BY TH' HAIR OF MY CHINNY-CHIN-CHIN!... I'VE GOT 'EM AT BAY, PIGS! WE WIN!
YEAH! ZEKE SAVED OUR BACON! WHO WOULDA THOUGHT?
HANDS UP!
BANG!
TH' SHERIFF?! BUT YOU SAID THIS WUZ LEGAL, BRER FOX!
QUIET, BEAR! I NEVER SAW YOU BE-FORE!
AND SO...
THANKEE, CITIZEN! LI'L WOLF TOLD ME EVERYTHING! YOU'RE A HERO...
AWW...!
...SAVIN' THE PIGS EVEN WHEN THEY'RE NO LONGER PROTECTED! KEEP IT UP, WOLF!
EH? NO LONGER—?!
SHERIFF GRIZZLY GOT THIS TELE-GRAM, POP!
"TAMWORTH NOT AT RISK... STOP... CALCULATION ERROR... STOP... CORRECT POPULATION ACTUALLY FOUR HUNDRED MILLION... STOP... STOP PROTECTION POLICY... STOP!"
HUH?
UH, OH! RUN FOR IT, BOYS!
FLEEIN'... AFTER I SAVED YA! SOME GRATITUDE!
HEH! BACK TO NATURE!
CAN'T SAY I MIND! AFTER THE SCARE WE HAD TODAY...
...WHO'S AFRAID OF THE BIG BAD WOLF?

WALT DISNEY'S MICKEY MOUSE IN MUMMY DEAREST _{PART TWO}

AT AN EXHIBITION OF THE FABULOUS *AMULET OF QUETCOATLZLE*, MINNIE IS STEAMED TO FIND MICKEY WITH THE EXOTIC BEAUTY, *LOTUS BLOSSOM*! WHEN THE AMULET VANISHES, MICKEY GOES SEARCHING FOR THE UNTRUSTWORTHY FEMME FATALE —

YER HUNCH WAS RIGHT, MINNIE! THAR HE IS!

MICKEY! ARE YOU OKAY?

OOOH! I WAS JUMPED BY A FANATICAL CULT! THEY ABSCONDED WITH THE AMULET AND BLOSSOM!

113

D 2002-243

YOU POOR DEAR! I KNOW THAT PIRATE QUEEN MEANS NOTHING TO YOU! AND NOW SHE'S OUT OF OUR HAIR!

I'M AFRAID NOT, MINNIE!

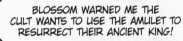

BLOSSOM WARNED ME THE CULT WANTS TO USE THE AMULET TO RESURRECT THEIR ANCIENT KING!

SHE SAID WHEN THAT MUMMY TAKES HIS THRONE ONCE AGAIN, IT'LL BRING ABOUT *THE END OF THE WORLD*!

YOU DON'T BELIEVE THAT, DO YOU?

I DON'T KNOW *WHAT* TO BELIEVE, BUT UNLESS BLOSSOM'S A BETTER ACTRESS THAN I THINK, SHE'S IN BIG TROUBLE!

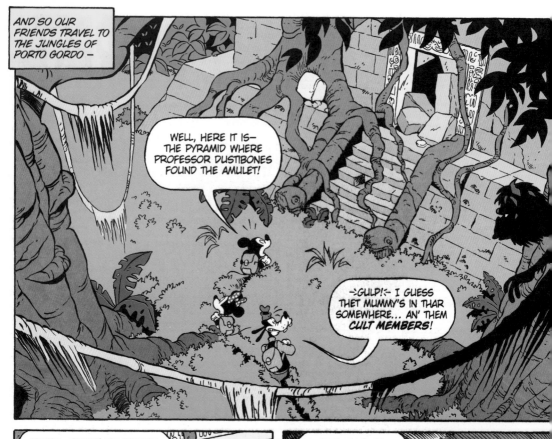

AND SO OUR FRIENDS TRAVEL TO THE JUNGLES OF PORTO GORDO —

WELL, HERE IT IS— THE PYRAMID WHERE PROFESSOR DUSTIBONES FOUND THE AMULET!

—⫶GULP!⫶— I GUESS THET MUMMY'S IN THAR SOMEWHERE... AN' THEM *CULT MEMBERS!*

LISTEN, MINNIE! I'D PREFER YOU WAIT OUT HERE!

AND LEAVE YOU TO BLUNDER INTO THE ARMS OF LOTUS BLOSSOM? *NEVER!*

OKAY! BUT KEEP BEHIND ME! WE DON'T KNOW WHAT WE'LL RUN INTO!

I JUS' HOPE THEM CULT CREEPS HAVEN'T HAD TIME TUH WAKE UP THET MUMMY YET!

I JUST HOPE LOTUS BLOSSOM'S ALL RIGHT!

HURMPH!

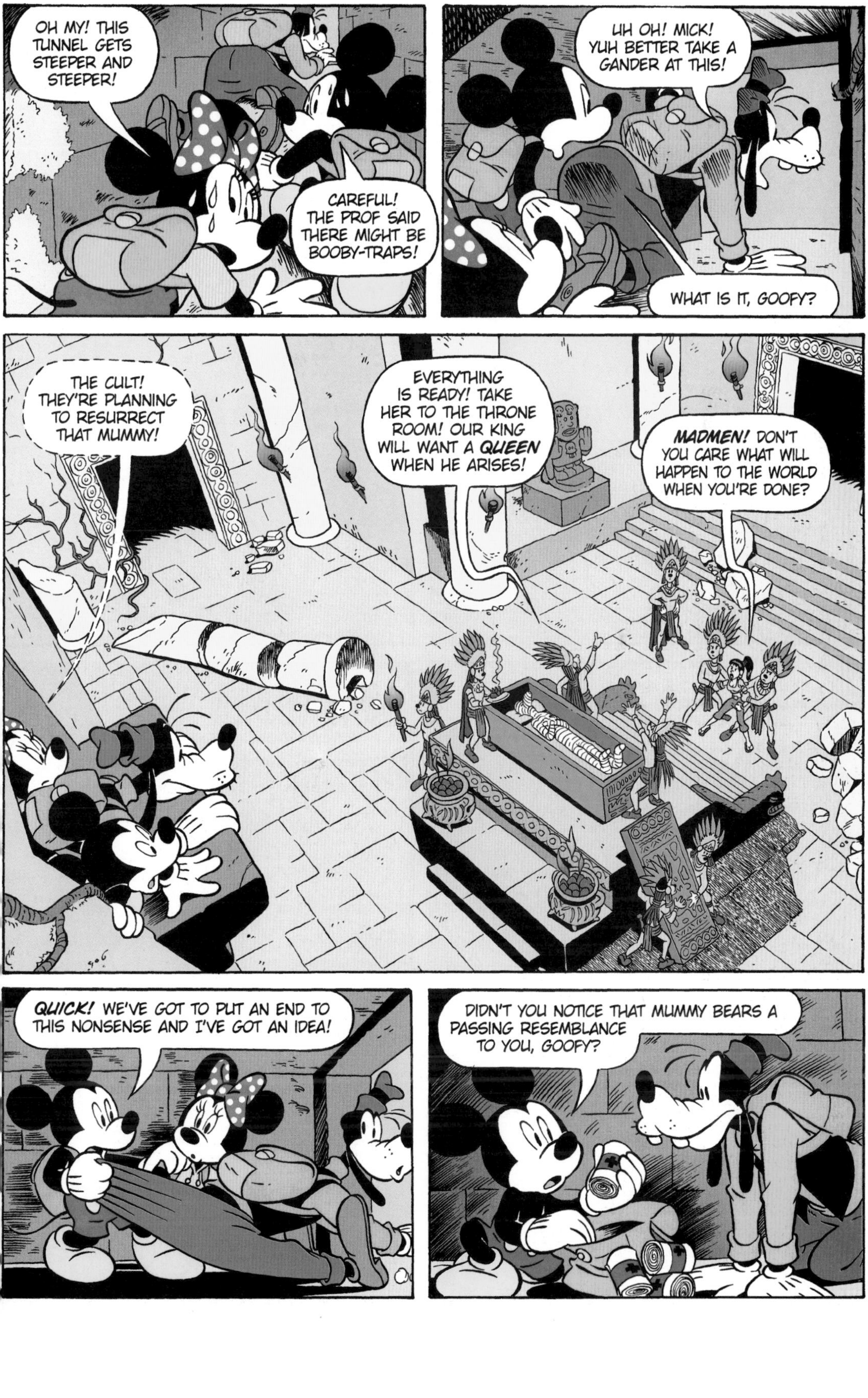
OH MY! THIS TUNNEL GETS STEEPER AND STEEPER!
CAREFUL! THE PROF SAID THERE MIGHT BE BOOBY-TRAPS!
UH OH! MICK! YUH BETTER TAKE A GANDER AT THIS!
WHAT IS IT, GOOFY?
THE CULT! THEY'RE PLANNING TO RESURRECT THAT MUMMY!
EVERYTHING IS READY! TAKE HER TO THE THRONE ROOM! OUR KING WILL WANT A QUEEN WHEN HE ARISES!
MADMEN! DON'T YOU CARE WHAT WILL HAPPEN TO THE WORLD WHEN YOU'RE DONE?
QUICK! WE'VE GOT TO PUT AN END TO THIS NONSENSE AND I'VE GOT AN IDEA!
DIDN'T YOU NOTICE THAT MUMMY BEARS A PASSING RESEMBLANCE TO YOU, GOOFY?

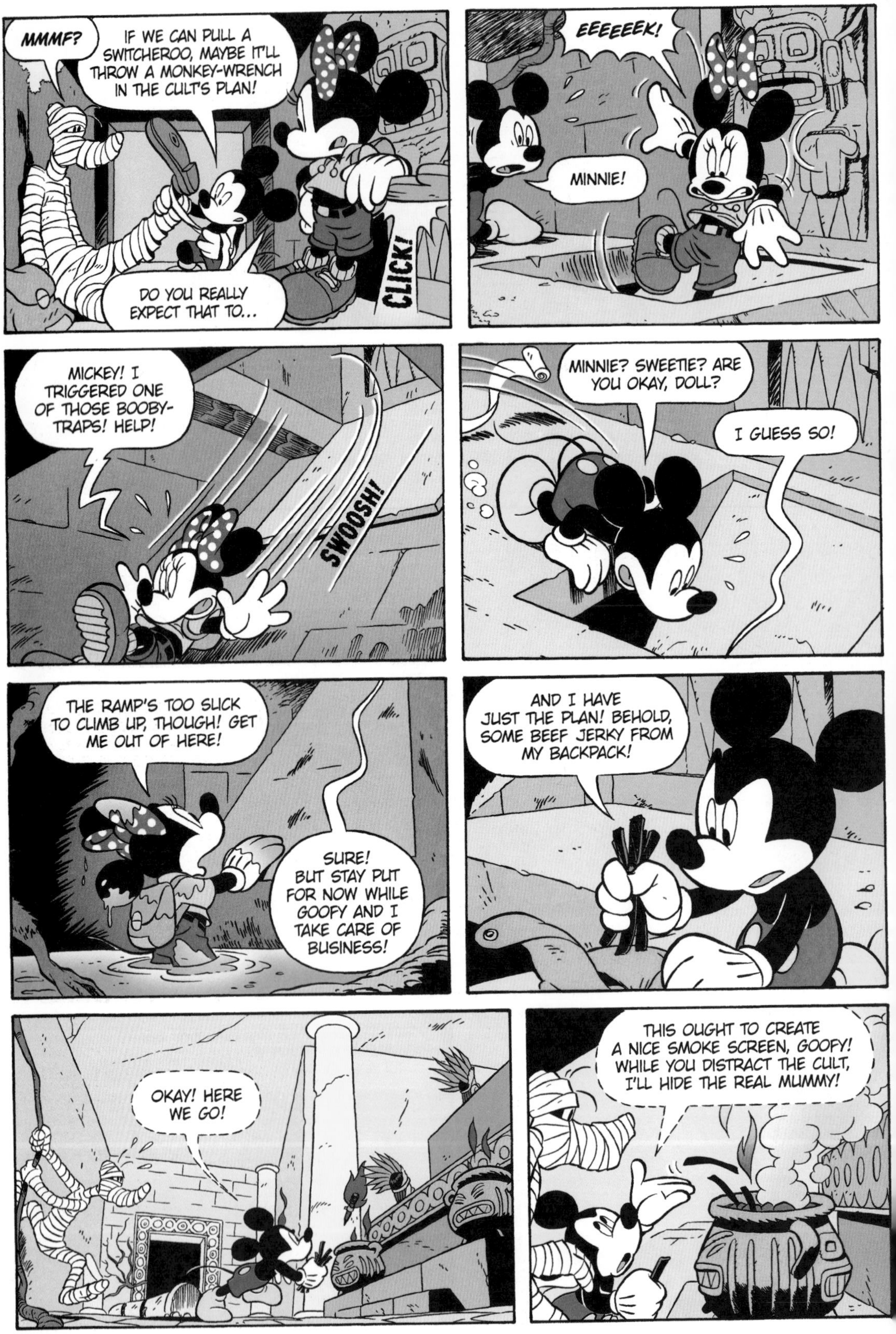
MMMF?
IF WE CAN PULL A SWITCHEROO, MAYBE IT'LL THROW A MONKEY-WRENCH IN THE CULT'S PLAN!
DO YOU REALLY EXPECT THAT TO...
CLICK!
EEEEEEK!
MINNIE!
MICKEY! I TRIGGERED ONE OF THOSE BOOBY-TRAPS! HELP!
SWOOSH!
MINNIE? SWEETIE? ARE YOU OKAY, DOLL?
I GUESS SO!
THE RAMP'S TOO SLICK TO CLIMB UP, THOUGH! GET ME OUT OF HERE!
SURE! BUT STAY PUT FOR NOW WHILE GOOFY AND I TAKE CARE OF BUSINESS!
AND I HAVE JUST THE PLAN! BEHOLD, SOME BEEF JERKY FROM MY BACKPACK!
OKAY! HERE WE GO!
THIS OUGHT TO CREATE A NICE SMOKE SCREEN, GOOFY! WHILE YOU DISTRACT THE CULT, I'LL HIDE THE REAL MUMMY!

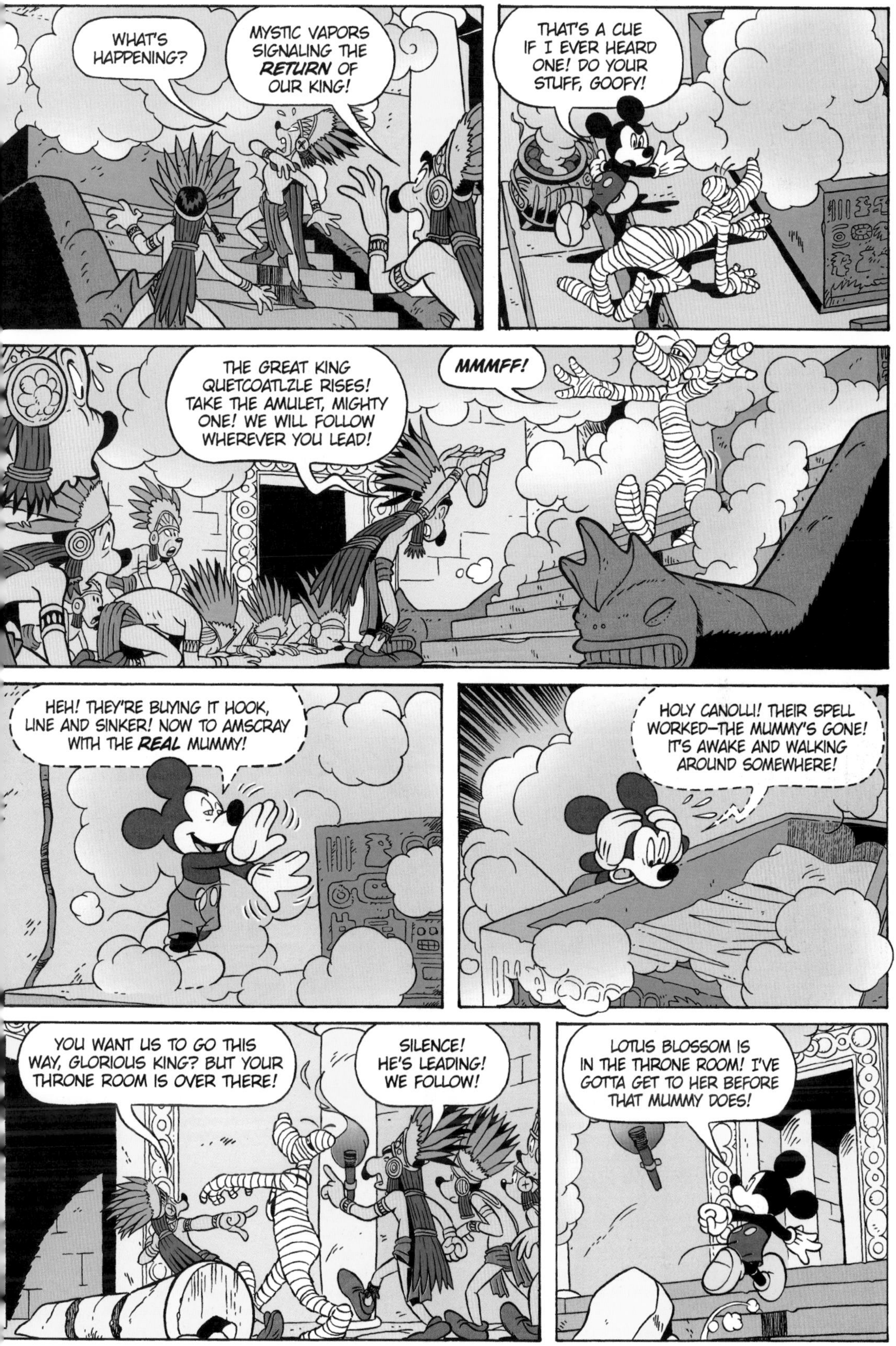
WHAT'S HAPPENING?
MYSTIC VAPORS SIGNALING THE RETURN OF OUR KING!
THAT'S A CUE IF I EVER HEARD ONE! DO YOUR STUFF, GOOFY!
THE GREAT KING QUETCOATLZLE RISES! TAKE THE AMULET, MIGHTY ONE! WE WILL FOLLOW WHEREVER YOU LEAD!
MMMFF!
HEH! THEY'RE BUYING IT HOOK, LINE AND SINKER! NOW TO AMSCRAY WITH THE REAL MUMMY!
HOLY CANOLLI! THEIR SPELL WORKED—THE MUMMY'S GONE! IT'S AWAKE AND WALKING AROUND SOMEWHERE!
YOU WANT US TO GO THIS WAY, GLORIOUS KING? BUT YOUR THRONE ROOM IS OVER THERE!
SILENCE! HE'S LEADING! WE FOLLOW!
LOTUS BLOSSOM IS IN THE THRONE ROOM! I'VE GOTTA GET TO HER BEFORE THAT MUMMY DOES!

BIG EARS! ARE YOU EVER A SIGHT FOR SORE EYES!

BLOSSOM! THANK FUDD YOU'RE OKAY! GUESS WHO'S BEEN RESURRECTED FROM THE DEAD?

I KNOW! WE NEED THE AMULET! IT CAN RETURN THE MUMMY TO ETERNAL SLEEP AS WELL AS AWAKEN HIM!

MEANWHILE —

I'M SICK OF WAITING AROUND DOWN HERE! I'LL FIND *MY OWN* WAY OUT! THIS CORRIDOR SHOULD DO...

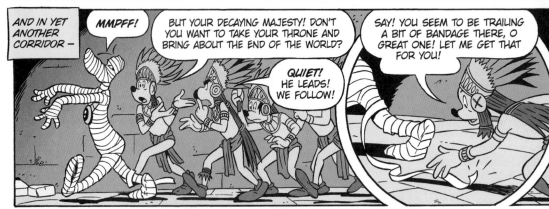

AND IN YET ANOTHER CORRIDOR —

MMPFF!

BUT YOUR DECAYING MAJESTY! DON'T YOU WANT TO TAKE YOUR THRONE AND BRING ABOUT THE END OF THE WORLD?

QUIET! HE LEADS! WE FOLLOW!

SAY! YOU SEEM TO BE TRAILING A BIT OF BANDAGE THERE, O GREAT ONE! LET ME GET THAT FOR YOU!

OH DEAR! THESE TUNNELS SPLIT OFF IN SEVERAL DIRECTIONS! WHICH WAY DO I GO TO FIND MICKEY AND GOOPY?

YEEAARGH!

EEEEK!

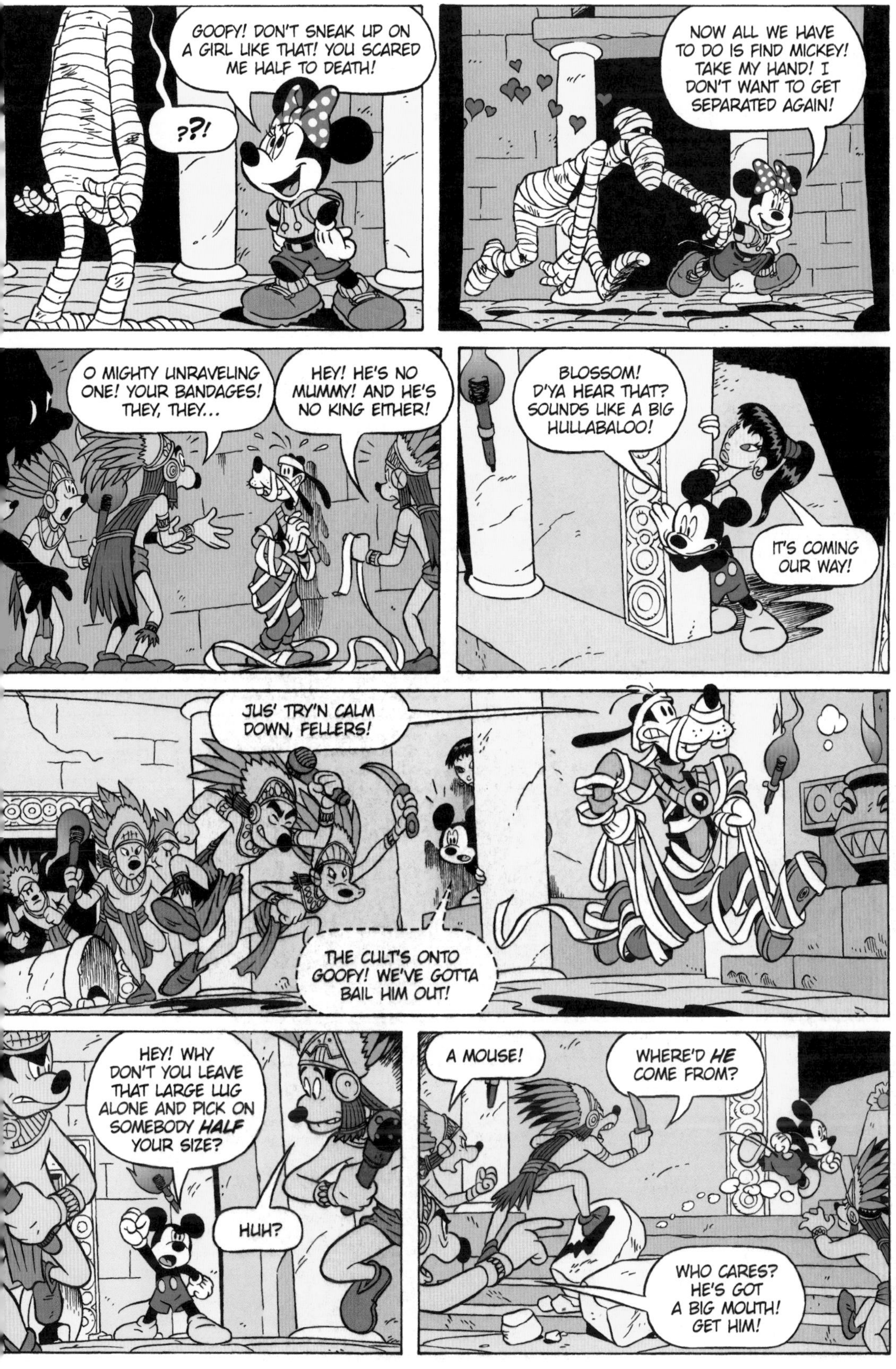
GOOFY! DON'T SNEAK UP ON A GIRL LIKE THAT! YOU SCARED ME HALF TO DEATH!
??!
NOW ALL WE HAVE TO DO IS FIND MICKEY! TAKE MY HAND! I DON'T WANT TO GET SEPARATED AGAIN!
O MIGHTY UNRAVELING ONE! YOUR BANDAGES! THEY, THEY...
HEY! HE'S NO MUMMY! AND HE'S NO KING EITHER!
BLOSSOM! D'YA HEAR THAT? SOUNDS LIKE A BIG HULLABALOO!
IT'S COMING OUR WAY!
JUS' TRY'N CALM DOWN, FELLERS!
THE CULT'S ONTO GOOFY! WE'VE GOTTA BAIL HIM OUT!
HEY! WHY DON'T YOU LEAVE THAT LARGE LUG ALONE AND PICK ON SOMEBODY HALF YOUR SIZE?
HUH?
A MOUSE!
WHERE'D HE COME FROM?
WHO CARES? HE'S GOT A BIG MOUTH! GET HIM!

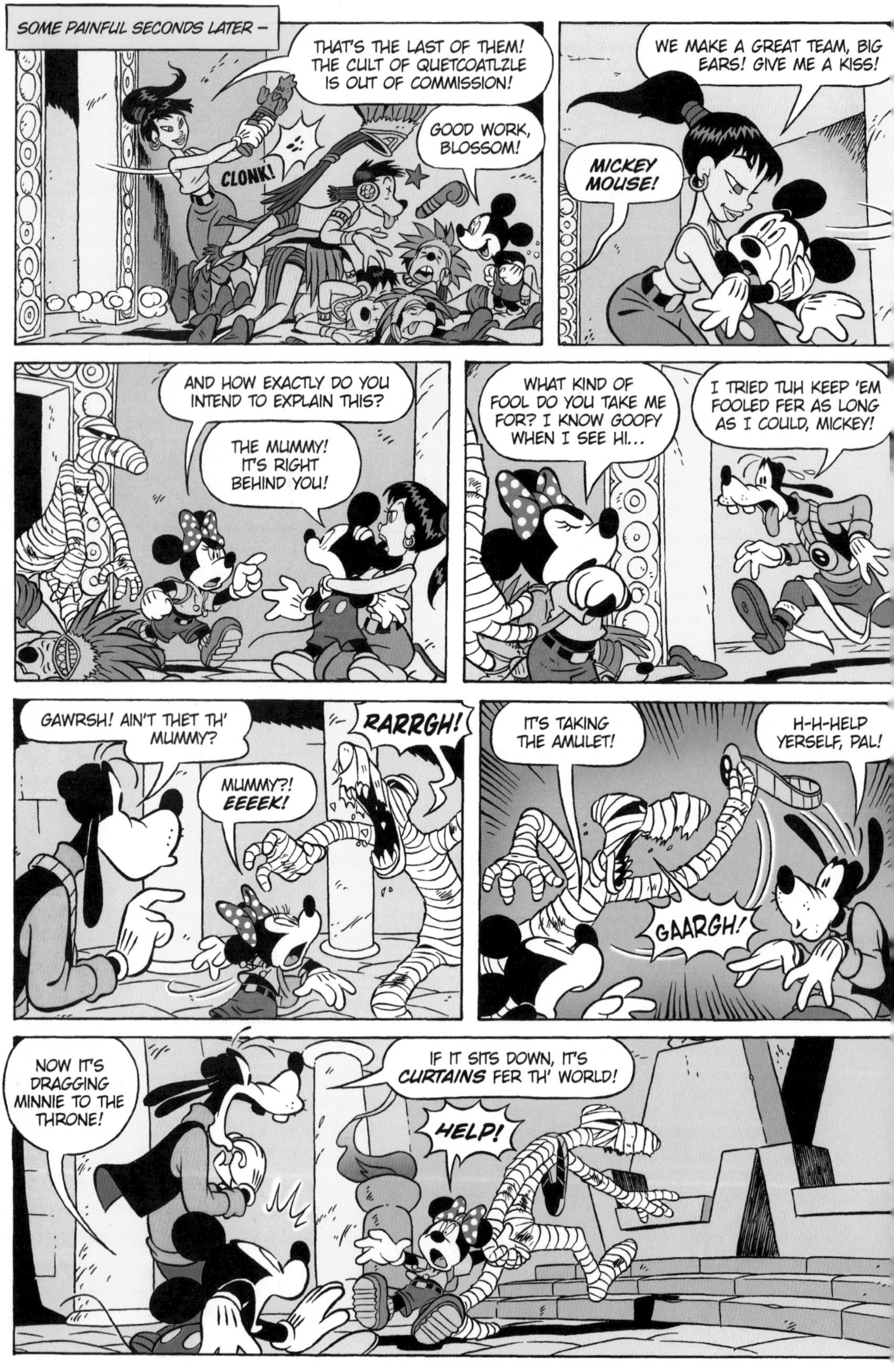

SOME PAINFUL SECONDS LATER –
THAT'S THE LAST OF THEM! THE CULT OF QUETCOATLZLE IS OUT OF COMMISSION!
CLONK!
GOOD WORK, BLOSSOM!
WE MAKE A GREAT TEAM, BIG EARS! GIVE ME A KISS!
MICKEY MOUSE!
AND HOW EXACTLY DO YOU INTEND TO EXPLAIN THIS?
THE MUMMY! IT'S RIGHT BEHIND YOU!
WHAT KIND OF FOOL DO YOU TAKE ME FOR? I KNOW GOOFY WHEN I SEE HI...
I TRIED TUH KEEP 'EM FOOLED FER AS LONG AS I COULD, MICKEY!
GAWRSH! AIN'T THET TH' MUMMY?
MUMMY?! EEEEK!
RARRGH!
IT'S TAKING THE AMULET!
H-H-HELP YERSELF, PAL!
GAARGH!
NOW IT'S DRAGGING MINNIE TO THE THRONE!
IF IT SITS DOWN, IT'S CURTAINS FER TH' WORLD!
HELP!

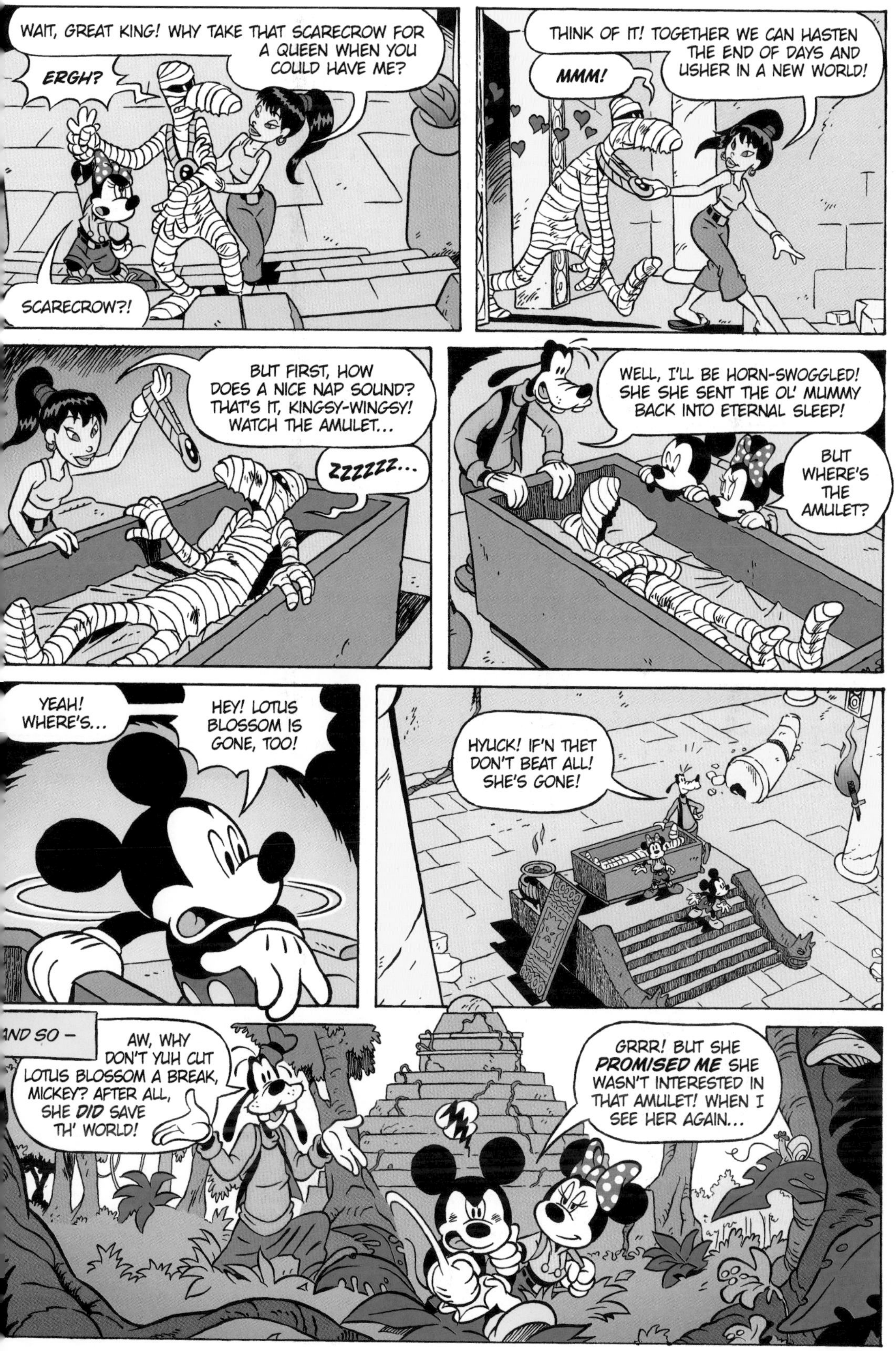
WAIT, GREAT KING! WHY TAKE THAT SCARECROW FOR A QUEEN WHEN YOU COULD HAVE ME?
ERGH?
SCARECROW?!
THINK OF IT! TOGETHER WE CAN HASTEN THE END OF DAYS AND USHER IN A NEW WORLD!
MMM!
BUT FIRST, HOW DOES A NICE NAP SOUND? THAT'S IT, KINGSY-WINGSY! WATCH THE AMULET...
ZZZZZZ...
WELL, I'LL BE HORN-SWOGGLED! SHE SHE SENT THE OL' MUMMY BACK INTO ETERNAL SLEEP!
BUT WHERE'S THE AMULET?
YEAH! WHERE'S...
HEY! LOTUS BLOSSOM IS GONE, TOO!
HYUCK! IF'N THET DON'T BEAT ALL! SHE'S GONE!
AND SO –
AW, WHY DON'T YUH CUT LOTUS BLOSSOM A BREAK, MICKEY? AFTER ALL, SHE DID SAVE TH' WORLD!
GRRR! BUT SHE PROMISED ME SHE WASN'T INTERESTED IN THAT AMULET! WHEN I SEE HER AGAIN...

THE END!

SCOOP

ATTRACTING YOUR FAVORITE CHARACTERS DAILY!

From SpongeBob to Superman, from Batman to Barbie, from Spider-Man to Snow White - with a power to rival Magneto, **Scoop** attracts all of your favorite comic characters! Loaded with magical, magnetic, marvelous morsels of info, this free weekly e-newsletter will pull you into a world of fun!

http://scoop.diamondgalleries.com

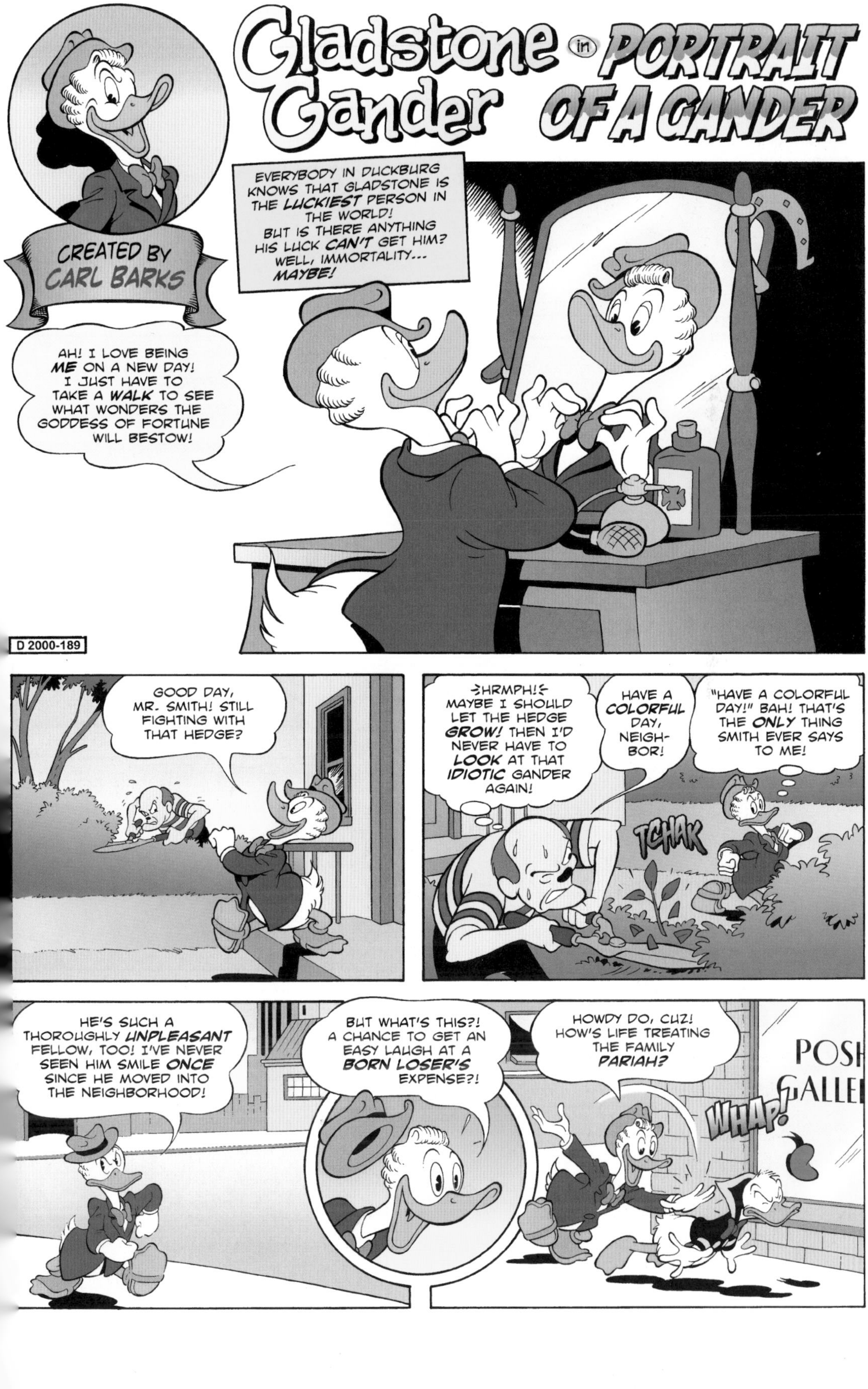

Gladstone Gander in PORTRAIT OF A GANDER
CREATED BY CARL BARKS
EVERYBODY IN DUCKBURG KNOWS THAT GLADSTONE IS THE LUCKIEST PERSON IN THE WORLD! BUT IS THERE ANYTHING HIS LUCK CAN'T GET HIM? WELL, IMMORTALITY... MAYBE!
AH! I LOVE BEING ME ON A NEW DAY! I JUST HAVE TO TAKE A WALK TO SEE WHAT WONDERS THE GODDESS OF FORTUNE WILL BESTOW!
D 2000-189
GOOD DAY, MR. SMITH! STILL FIGHTING WITH THAT HEDGE?
HRMPH! MAYBE I SHOULD LET THE HEDGE GROW! THEN I'D NEVER HAVE TO LOOK AT THAT IDIOTIC GANDER AGAIN!
HAVE A COLORFUL DAY, NEIGH-BOR!
"HAVE A COLORFUL DAY!" BAH! THAT'S THE ONLY THING SMITH EVER SAYS TO ME!
TCHAK
HE'S SUCH A THOROUGHLY UNPLEASANT FELLOW, TOO! I'VE NEVER SEEN HIM SMILE ONCE SINCE HE MOVED INTO THE NEIGHBORHOOD!
BUT WHAT'S THIS?! A CHANCE TO GET AN EASY LAUGH AT A BORN LOSER'S EXPENSE?!
HOWDY DO, CUZ! HOW'S LIFE TREATING THE FAMILY PARIAH?
WHAP!
POSH GALLE

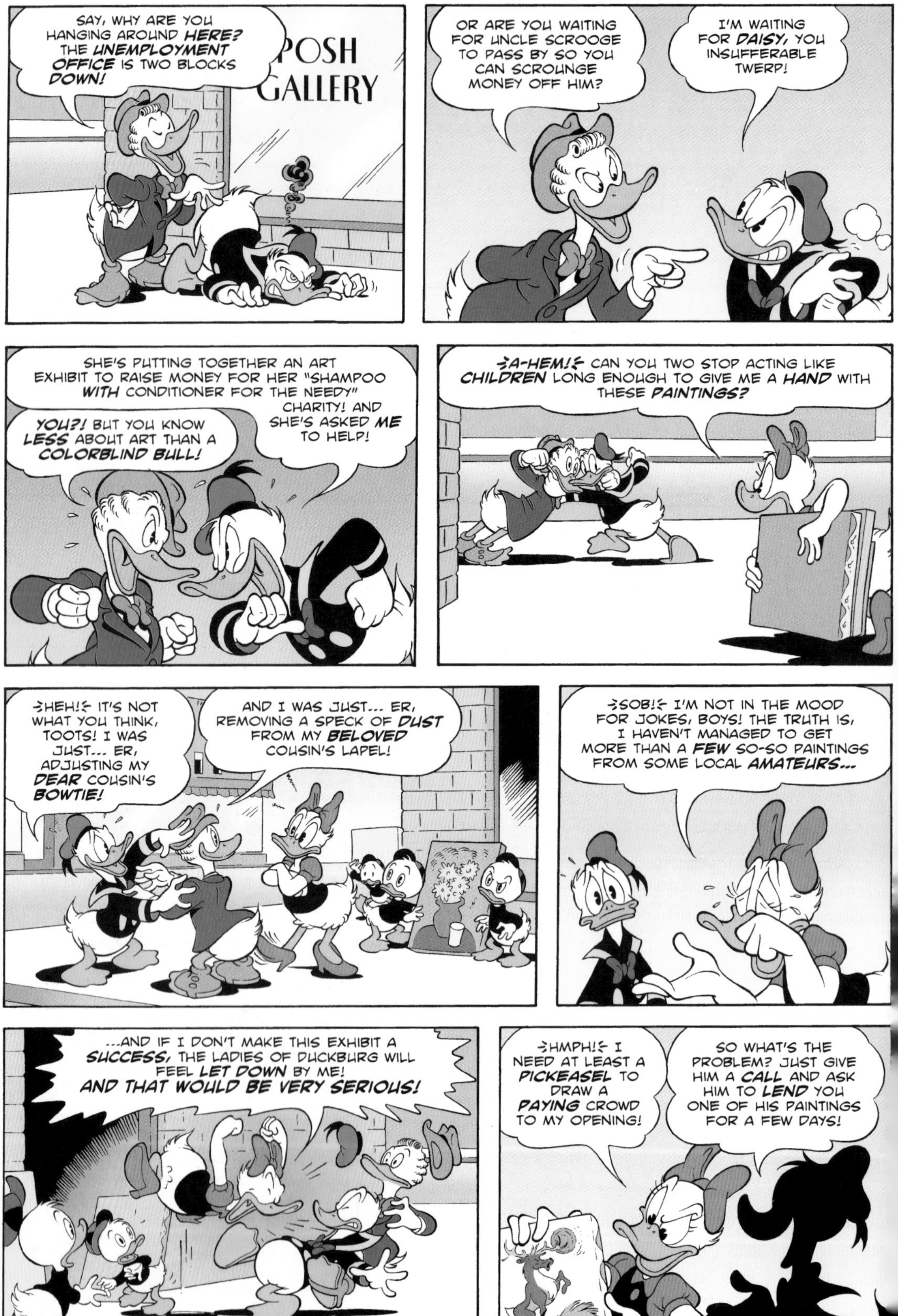
SAY, WHY ARE YOU HANGING AROUND HERE? THE UNEMPLOYMENT OFFICE IS TWO BLOCKS DOWN!
POSH GALLERY
OR ARE YOU WAITING FOR UNCLE SCROOGE TO PASS BY SO YOU CAN SCROUNGE MONEY OFF HIM?
I'M WAITING FOR DAISY, YOU INSUFFERABLE TWERP!
SHE'S PUTTING TOGETHER AN ART EXHIBIT TO RAISE MONEY FOR HER "SHAMPOO WITH CONDITIONER FOR THE NEEDY" CHARITY! AND SHE'S ASKED ME TO HELP!
YOU?! BUT YOU KNOW LESS ABOUT ART THAN A COLORBLIND BULL!
A-HEM! CAN YOU TWO STOP ACTING LIKE CHILDREN LONG ENOUGH TO GIVE ME A HAND WITH THESE PAINTINGS?
HEH! IT'S NOT WHAT YOU THINK, TOOTS! I WAS JUST... ER, ADJUSTING MY DEAR COUSIN'S BOWTIE!
AND I WAS JUST... ER, REMOVING A SPECK OF DUST FROM MY BELOVED COUSIN'S LAPEL!
SOB! I'M NOT IN THE MOOD FOR JOKES, BOYS! THE TRUTH IS, I HAVEN'T MANAGED TO GET MORE THAN A FEW SO-SO PAINTINGS FROM SOME LOCAL AMATEURS...
...AND IF I DON'T MAKE THIS EXHIBIT A SUCCESS, THE LADIES OF DUCKBURG WILL FEEL LET DOWN BY ME! AND THAT WOULD BE VERY SERIOUS!
HMPH! I NEED AT LEAST A PICKEASEL TO DRAW A PAYING CROWD TO MY OPENING!
SO WHAT'S THE PROBLEM? JUST GIVE HIM A CALL AND ASK HIM TO LEND YOU ONE OF HIS PAINTINGS FOR A FEW DAYS!

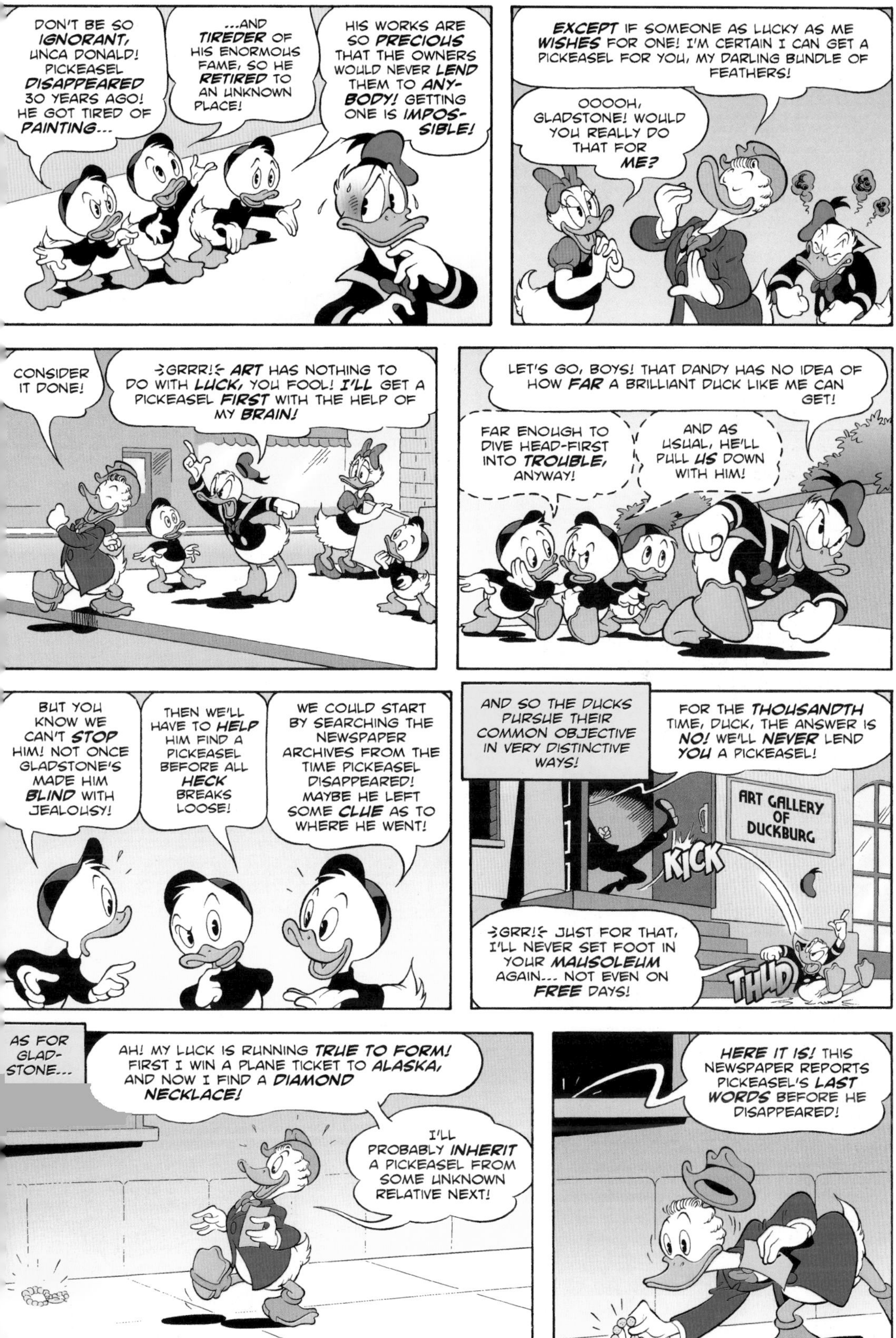

DON'T BE SO IGNORANT, UNCA DONALD! PICKEASEL DISAPPEARED 30 YEARS AGO! HE GOT TIRED OF PAINTING...
...AND TIREDER OF HIS ENORMOUS FAME, SO HE RETIRED TO AN UNKNOWN PLACE!
HIS WORKS ARE SO PRECIOUS THAT THE OWNERS WOULD NEVER LEND THEM TO ANYBODY! GETTING ONE IS IMPOSSIBLE!
EXCEPT IF SOMEONE AS LUCKY AS ME WISHES FOR ONE! I'M CERTAIN I CAN GET A PICKEASEL FOR YOU, MY DARLING BUNDLE OF FEATHERS!
OOOOH, GLADSTONE! WOULD YOU REALLY DO THAT FOR ME?
CONSIDER IT DONE!
GRRR! ART HAS NOTHING TO DO WITH LUCK, YOU FOOL! I'LL GET A PICKEASEL FIRST WITH THE HELP OF MY BRAIN!
LET'S GO, BOYS! THAT DANDY HAS NO IDEA OF HOW FAR A BRILLIANT DUCK LIKE ME CAN GET!
FAR ENOUGH TO DIVE HEAD-FIRST INTO TROUBLE, ANYWAY!
AND AS USUAL, HE'LL PULL US DOWN WITH HIM!
BUT YOU KNOW WE CAN'T STOP HIM! NOT ONCE GLADSTONE'S MADE HIM BLIND WITH JEALOUSY!
THEN WE'LL HAVE TO HELP HIM FIND A PICKEASEL BEFORE ALL HECK BREAKS LOOSE!
WE COULD START BY SEARCHING THE NEWSPAPER ARCHIVES FROM THE TIME PICKEASEL DISAPPEARED! MAYBE HE LEFT SOME CLUE AS TO WHERE HE WENT!
AND SO THE DUCKS PURSUE THEIR COMMON OBJECTIVE IN VERY DISTINCTIVE WAYS!
FOR THE THOUSANDTH TIME, DUCK, THE ANSWER IS NO! WE'LL NEVER LEND YOU A PICKEASEL!
ART GALLERY OF DUCKBURG
KICK
GRR! JUST FOR THAT, I'LL NEVER SET FOOT IN YOUR MAUSOLEUM AGAIN... NOT EVEN ON FREE DAYS!
THUD
AS FOR GLADSTONE...
AH! MY LUCK IS RUNNING TRUE TO FORM! FIRST I WIN A PLANE TICKET TO ALASKA, AND NOW I FIND A DIAMOND NECKLACE!
I'LL PROBABLY INHERIT A PICKEASEL FROM SOME UNKNOWN RELATIVE NEXT!
HERE IT IS! THIS NEWSPAPER REPORTS PICKEASEL'S LAST WORDS BEFORE HE DISAPPEARED!

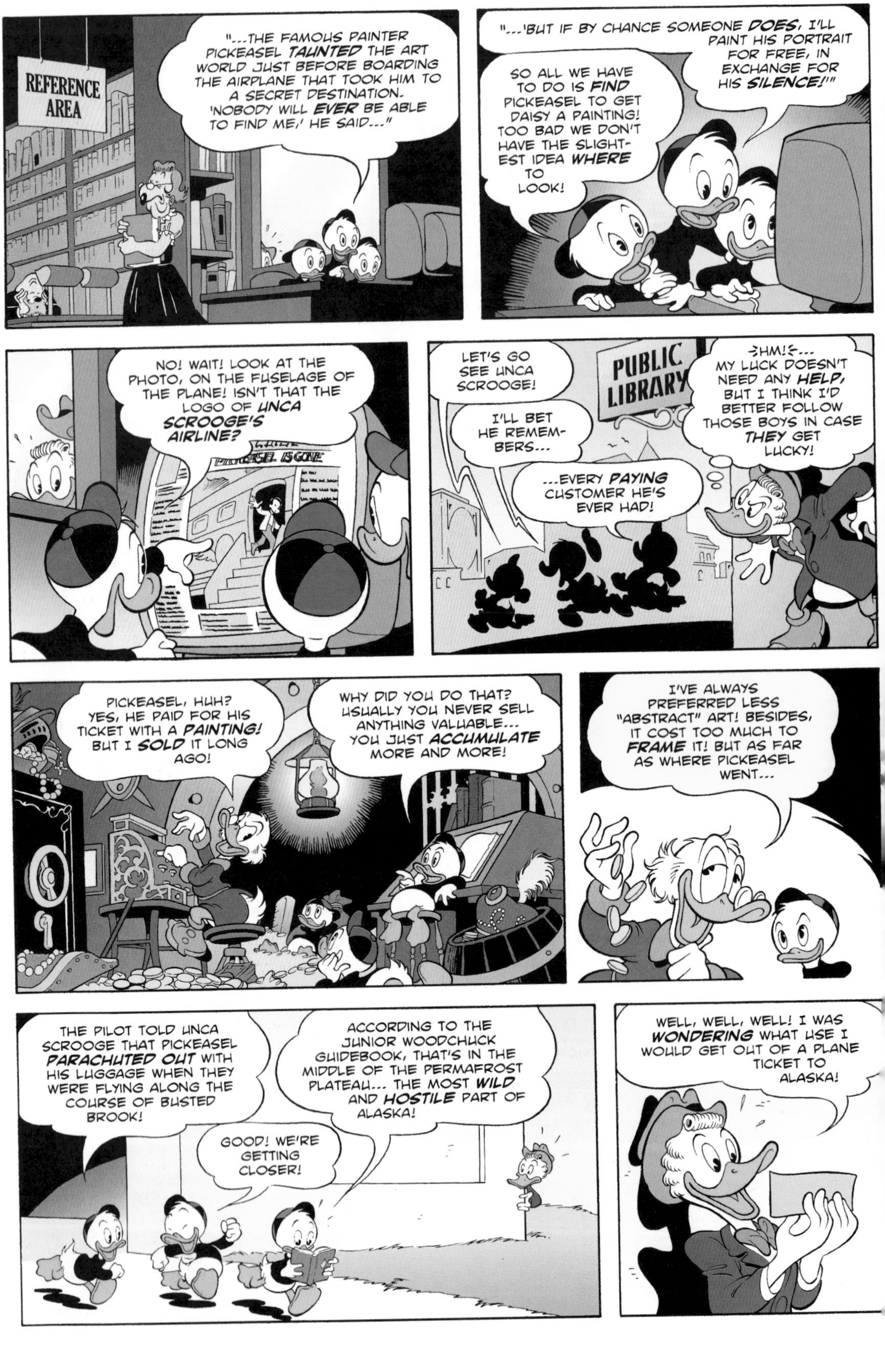
REFERENCE AREA
"...THE FAMOUS PAINTER PICKEASEL TAUNTED THE ART WORLD JUST BEFORE BOARDING THE AIRPLANE THAT TOOK HIM TO A SECRET DESTINATION. 'NOBODY WILL EVER BE ABLE TO FIND ME,' HE SAID..."
"...'BUT IF BY CHANCE SOMEONE DOES, I'LL PAINT HIS PORTRAIT FOR FREE, IN EXCHANGE FOR HIS SILENCE!'"
SO ALL WE HAVE TO DO IS FIND PICKEASEL TO GET DAISY A PAINTING! TOO BAD WE DON'T HAVE THE SLIGHT-EST IDEA WHERE TO LOOK!
NO! WAIT! LOOK AT THE PHOTO, ON THE FUSELAGE OF THE PLANE! ISN'T THAT THE LOGO OF UNCA SCROOGE'S AIRLINE?
PICKEASEL IS GONE
LET'S GO SEE UNCA SCROOGE!
PUBLIC LIBRARY
I'LL BET HE REMEM-BERS...
...EVERY PAYING CUSTOMER HE'S EVER HAD!
HM!... MY LUCK DOESN'T NEED ANY HELP, BUT I THINK I'D BETTER FOLLOW THOSE BOYS IN CASE THEY GET LUCKY!
PICKEASEL, HUH? YES, HE PAID FOR HIS TICKET WITH A PAINTING! BUT I SOLD IT LONG AGO!
WHY DID YOU DO THAT? USUALLY YOU NEVER SELL ANYTHING VALUABLE... YOU JUST ACCUMULATE MORE AND MORE!
I'VE ALWAYS PREFERRED LESS "ABSTRACT" ART! BESIDES, IT COST TOO MUCH TO FRAME IT! BUT AS FAR AS WHERE PICKEASEL WENT...
THE PILOT TOLD UNCA SCROOGE THAT PICKEASEL PARACHUTED OUT WITH HIS LUGGAGE WHEN THEY WERE FLYING ALONG THE COURSE OF BUSTED BROOK!
ACCORDING TO THE JUNIOR WOODCHUCK GUIDEBOOK, THAT'S IN THE MIDDLE OF THE PERMAFROST PLATEAU... THE MOST WILD AND HOSTILE PART OF ALASKA!
GOOD! WE'RE GETTING CLOSER!
WELL, WELL, WELL! I WAS WONDERING WHAT USE I WOULD GET OUT OF A PLANE TICKET TO ALASKA!

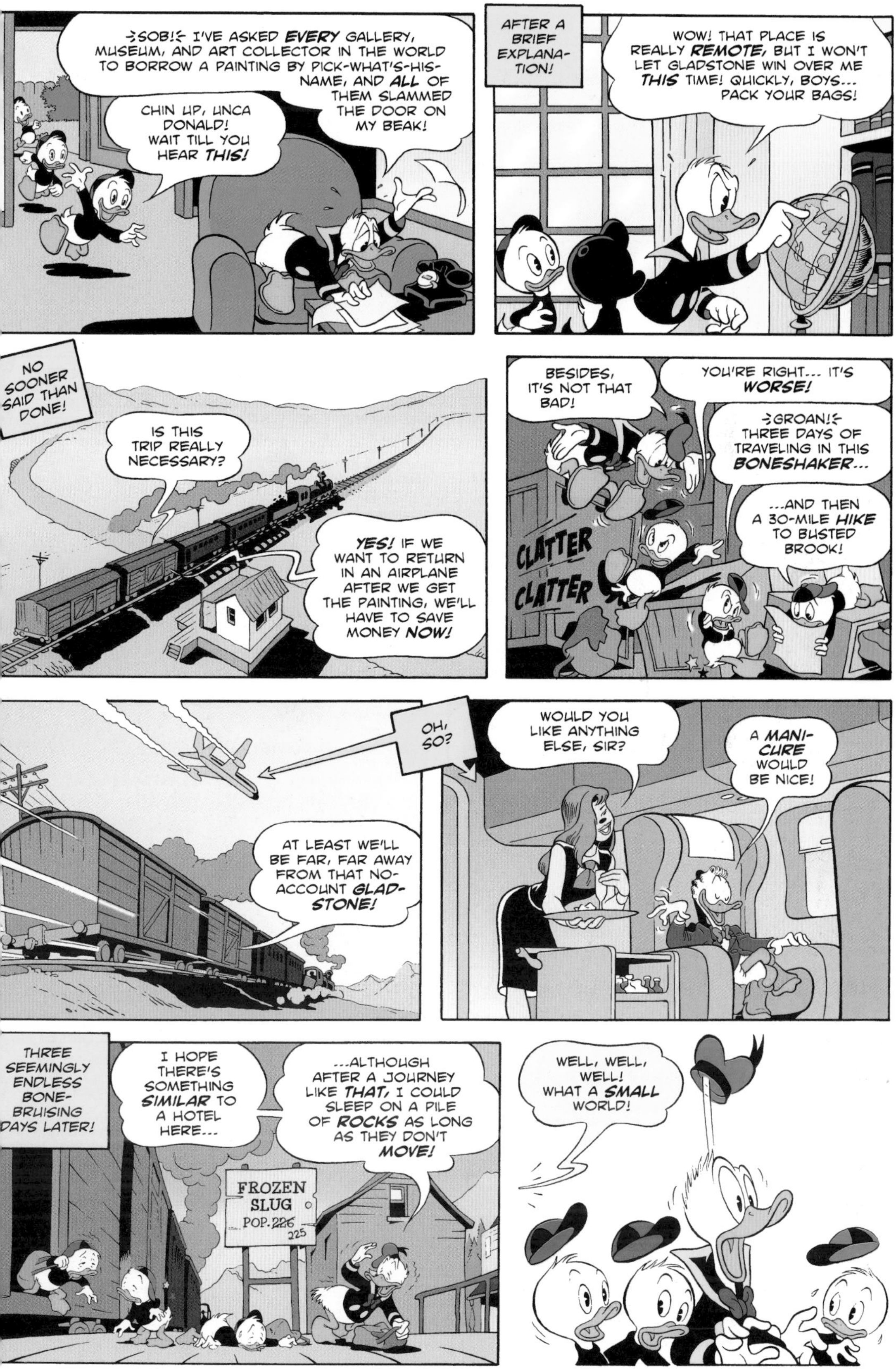

SOB! I'VE ASKED EVERY GALLERY, MUSEUM, AND ART COLLECTOR IN THE WORLD TO BORROW A PAINTING BY PICK-WHAT'S-HIS-NAME, AND ALL OF THEM SLAMMED THE DOOR ON MY BEAK!
CHIN UP, UNCA DONALD! WAIT TILL YOU HEAR THIS!
AFTER A BRIEF EXPLANATION!
WOW! THAT PLACE IS REALLY REMOTE, BUT I WON'T LET GLADSTONE WIN OVER ME THIS TIME! QUICKLY, BOYS... PACK YOUR BAGS!
NO SOONER SAID THAN DONE!
IS THIS TRIP REALLY NECESSARY?
YES! IF WE WANT TO RETURN IN AN AIRPLANE AFTER WE GET THE PAINTING, WE'LL HAVE TO SAVE MONEY NOW!
BESIDES, IT'S NOT THAT BAD!
YOU'RE RIGHT... IT'S WORSE!
GROAN! THREE DAYS OF TRAVELING IN THIS BONESHAKER...
...AND THEN A 30-MILE HIKE TO BUSTED BROOK!
CLATTER
CLATTER
OH, SO?
AT LEAST WE'LL BE FAR, FAR AWAY FROM THAT NO-ACCOUNT GLADSTONE!
WOULD YOU LIKE ANYTHING ELSE, SIR?
A MANICURE WOULD BE NICE!
THREE SEEMINGLY ENDLESS BONE-BRUISING DAYS LATER!
I HOPE THERE'S SOMETHING SIMILAR TO A HOTEL HERE...
...ALTHOUGH AFTER A JOURNEY LIKE THAT, I COULD SLEEP ON A PILE OF ROCKS AS LONG AS THEY DON'T MOVE!
FROZEN SLUG
POP. 226 225
WELL, WELL, WELL! WHAT A SMALL WORLD!

MY, MY... DON'T YOU LOOK AWFUL, CUZ! I TAKE IT YOU DIDN'T FLY UP HERE FIRST CLASS?
GRROAAR! GRRAAOOO-OOOORRR! GRRR!
QUICK! CHECK THE WOODCHUCK GUIDEBOOK TO SEE IF COUSIN-BASHING IS ILLEGAL IN ALASKA!
DOESN'T SEEM TO BE...
LET HIM GO THEN!
THAT NIGHT, AT FROZEN SLUG'S ONLY "HOTEL"!
YOU TWO ARE RIDICULOUS! YOU SHOULD JOIN FORCES TO HELP DAISY, NOT FIGHT OVER WHO'S LEAST PATHETIC!
ALL RIGHT, ALL RIGHT! PICKEASEL PARACHUTED DOWN SOMEWHERE ALONG BUSTED BROOK, BUT THAT'S A LOT OF ACREAGE TO SEARCH!
YOU'RE GRUMBLE WELCOME TO HELP, GLADSTONE!
MORE SOUP, LITTLE ONE?
EXCUSE ME, MA'AM! WHO MADE THE DRAWING ON THAT SOUP POT?
JUST SOME HERMIT WHO LIVES ON TOP OF MOUNT MISERY! HE USED TO COME DOWN A COUPLE OF TIMES A YEAR TO BUY PROVISIONS, BUT IT'S BEEN A WHILE SINCE HE'S BEEN AROUND!
PICKEAS-EL?!
THAT DRAWING IS DEFINITELY A PICKEASEL! MAYBE WE COULD BORROW THE POT...
NO! WE CAME LOOKING FOR A PAINTING! BESIDES, HE DIDN'T SIGN IT!
SO, BRIGHT AND EARLY THE NEXT MORNING...
SLUDGE BED HOTEL
ARE YOU SURE YOU'RE NOT COMING WITH US, GLADSTONE?
POSITIVE! HIKING IS TOO MUCH LIKE... WORK! I'LL TRUST MY LUCK TO GET ME THERE FIRST!

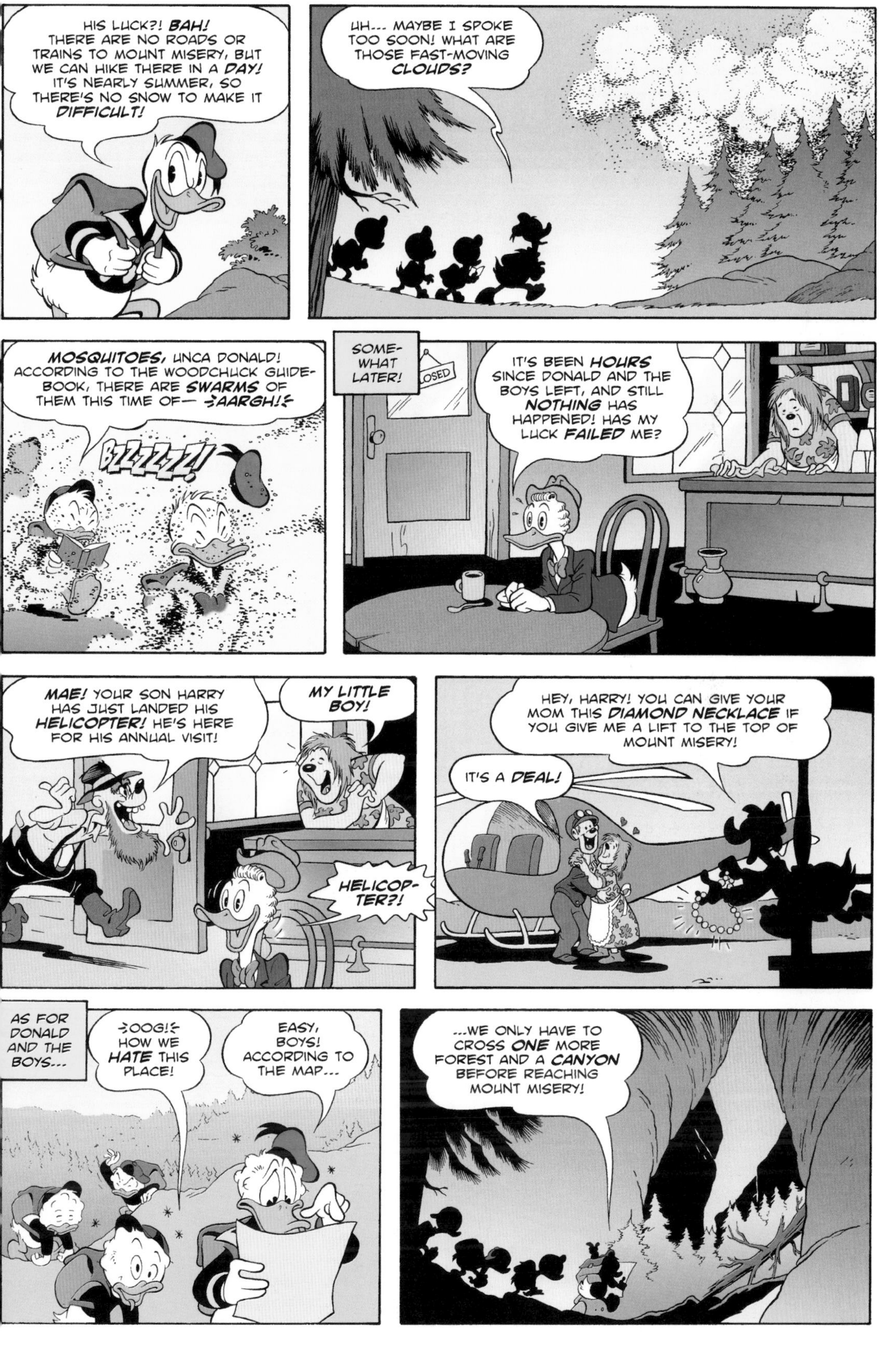

HIS LUCK?! BAH! THERE ARE NO ROADS OR TRAINS TO MOUNT MISERY, BUT WE CAN HIKE THERE IN A DAY! IT'S NEARLY SUMMER, SO THERE'S NO SNOW TO MAKE IT DIFFICULT!
UH... MAYBE I SPOKE TOO SOON! WHAT ARE THOSE FAST-MOVING CLOUDS?
MOSQUITOES, UNCA DONALD! ACCORDING TO THE WOODCHUCK GUIDE-BOOK, THERE ARE SWARMS OF THEM THIS TIME OF— AARGH!
BZZZZZZ!
SOME-WHAT LATER!
OSED
IT'S BEEN HOURS SINCE DONALD AND THE BOYS LEFT, AND STILL NOTHING HAS HAPPENED! HAS MY LUCK FAILED ME?
MAE! YOUR SON HARRY HAS JUST LANDED HIS HELICOPTER! HE'S HERE FOR HIS ANNUAL VISIT!
MY LITTLE BOY!
HELICOP-TER?!
HEY, HARRY! YOU CAN GIVE YOUR MOM THIS DIAMOND NECKLACE IF YOU GIVE ME A LIFT TO THE TOP OF MOUNT MISERY!
IT'S A DEAL!
AS FOR DONALD AND THE BOYS...
OOG! HOW WE HATE THIS PLACE!
EASY, BOYS! ACCORDING TO THE MAP...
...WE ONLY HAVE TO CROSS ONE MORE FOREST AND A CANYON BEFORE REACHING MOUNT MISERY!

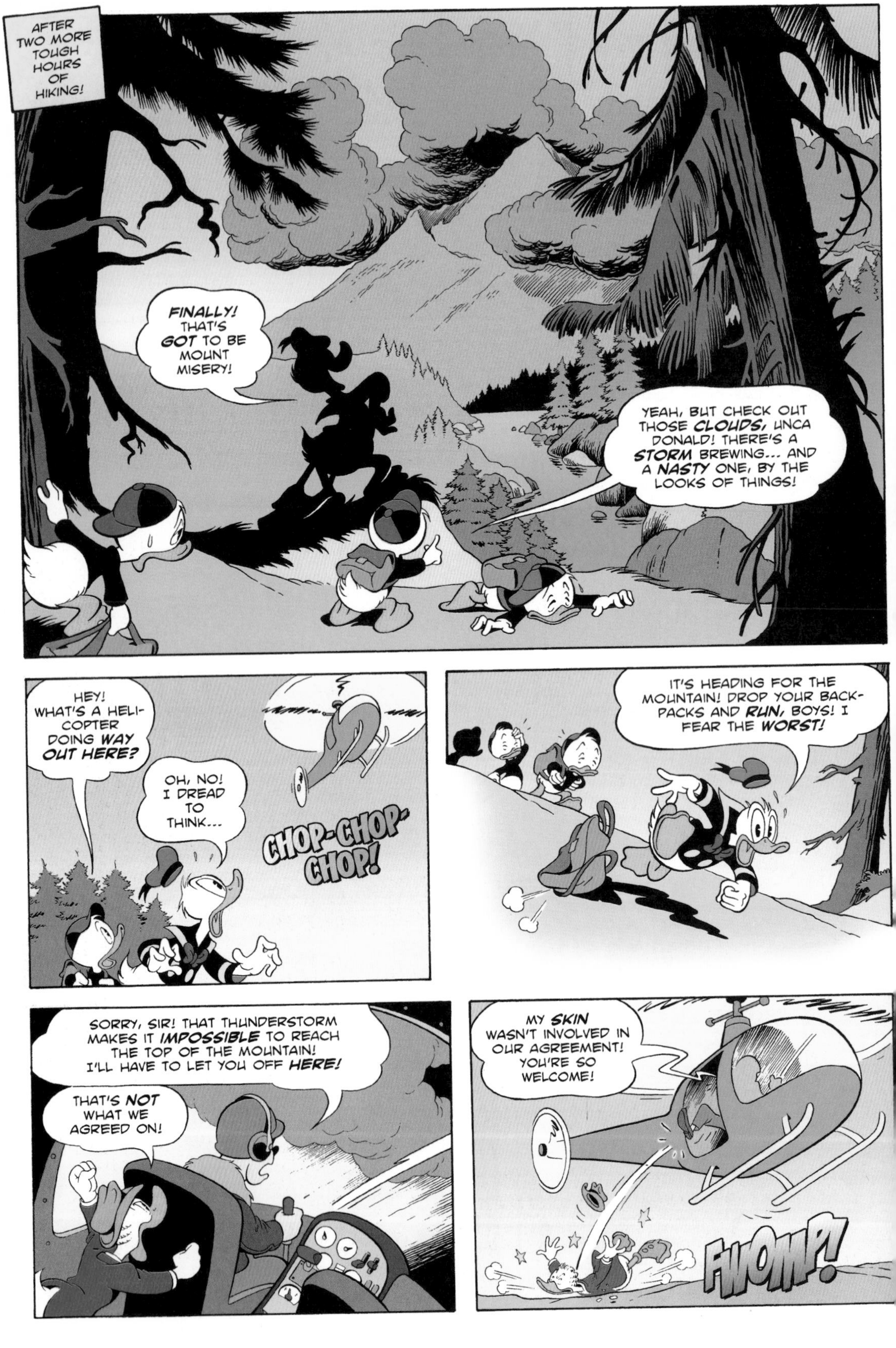
AFTER TWO MORE TOUGH HOURS OF HIKING!
FINALLY! THAT'S GOT TO BE MOUNT MISERY!
YEAH, BUT CHECK OUT THOSE CLOUDS, UNCA DONALD! THERE'S A STORM BREWING... AND A NASTY ONE, BY THE LOOKS OF THINGS!
HEY! WHAT'S A HELI-COPTER DOING WAY OUT HERE?
OH, NO! I DREAD TO THINK...
CHOP-CHOP-CHOP!
IT'S HEADING FOR THE MOUNTAIN! DROP YOUR BACK-PACKS AND RUN, BOYS! I FEAR THE WORST!
SORRY, SIR! THAT THUNDERSTORM MAKES IT IMPOSSIBLE TO REACH THE TOP OF THE MOUNTAIN! I'LL HAVE TO LET YOU OFF HERE!
THAT'S NOT WHAT WE AGREED ON!
MY SKIN WASN'T INVOLVED IN OUR AGREEMENT! YOU'RE SO WELCOME!
FWOMP!

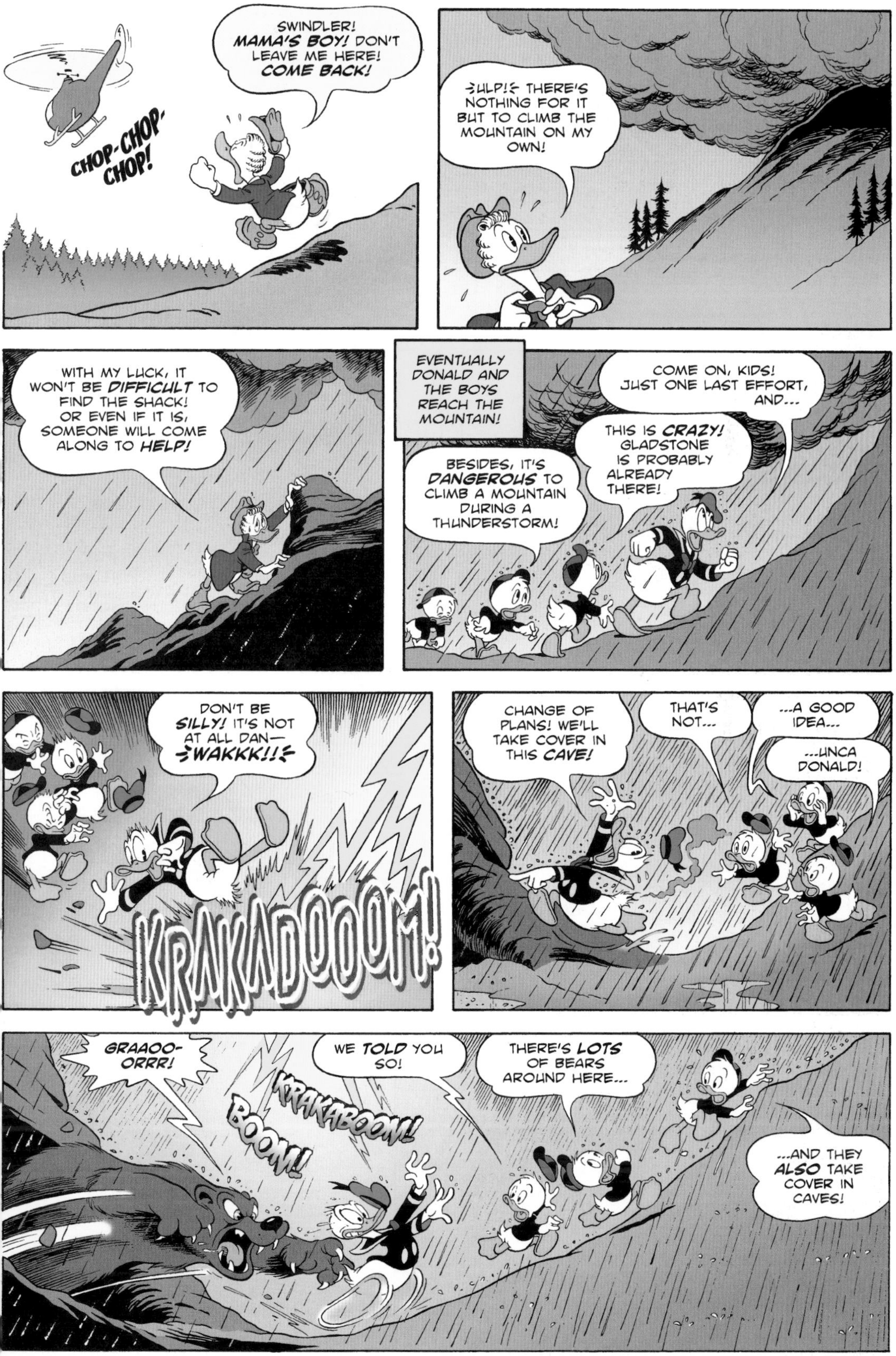

SWINDLER! MAMA'S BOY! DON'T LEAVE ME HERE! COME BACK!
CHOP-CHOP-CHOP!
ULP! THERE'S NOTHING FOR IT BUT TO CLIMB THE MOUNTAIN ON MY OWN!
WITH MY LUCK, IT WON'T BE DIFFICULT TO FIND THE SHACK! OR EVEN IF IT IS, SOMEONE WILL COME ALONG TO HELP!
EVENTUALLY DONALD AND THE BOYS REACH THE MOUNTAIN!
COME ON, KIDS! JUST ONE LAST EFFORT, AND...
THIS IS CRAZY! GLADSTONE IS PROBABLY ALREADY THERE!
BESIDES, IT'S DANGEROUS TO CLIMB A MOUNTAIN DURING A THUNDERSTORM!
DON'T BE SILLY! IT'S NOT AT ALL DAN— WAKKK!!
KRAKADOOOM!
CHANGE OF PLANS! WE'LL TAKE COVER IN THIS CAVE!
THAT'S NOT...
...A GOOD IDEA...
...UNCA DONALD!
GRAAOO-ORRR!
WE TOLD YOU SO!
KRAKABOOM!
BOOM!
THERE'S LOTS OF BEARS AROUND HERE...
...AND THEY ALSO TAKE COVER IN CAVES!

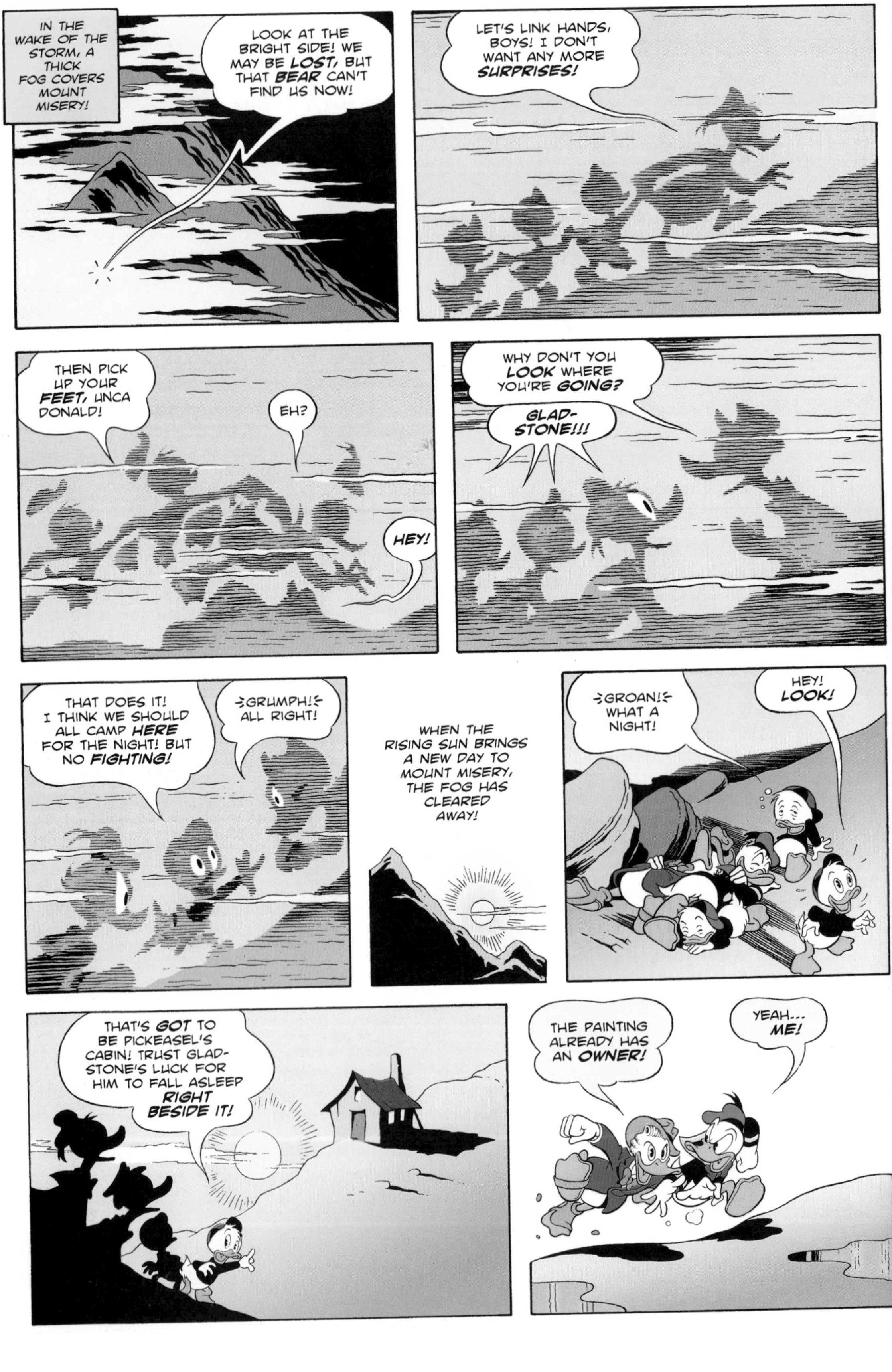

IN THE WAKE OF THE STORM, A THICK FOG COVERS MOUNT MISERY!
LOOK AT THE BRIGHT SIDE! WE MAY BE LOST, BUT THAT BEAR CAN'T FIND US NOW!
LET'S LINK HANDS, BOYS! I DON'T WANT ANY MORE SURPRISES!
THEN PICK UP YOUR FEET, UNCA DONALD!
EH?
HEY!
WHY DON'T YOU LOOK WHERE YOU'RE GOING?
GLAD-STONE!!!
THAT DOES IT! I THINK WE SHOULD ALL CAMP HERE FOR THE NIGHT! BUT NO FIGHTING!
GRUMPH! ALL RIGHT!
WHEN THE RISING SUN BRINGS A NEW DAY TO MOUNT MISERY, THE FOG HAS CLEARED AWAY!
GROAN! WHAT A NIGHT!
HEY! LOOK!
THAT'S GOT TO BE PICKEASEL'S CABIN! TRUST GLAD-STONE'S LUCK FOR HIM TO FALL ASLEEP RIGHT BESIDE IT!
THE PAINTING ALREADY HAS AN OWNER!
YEAH... ME!

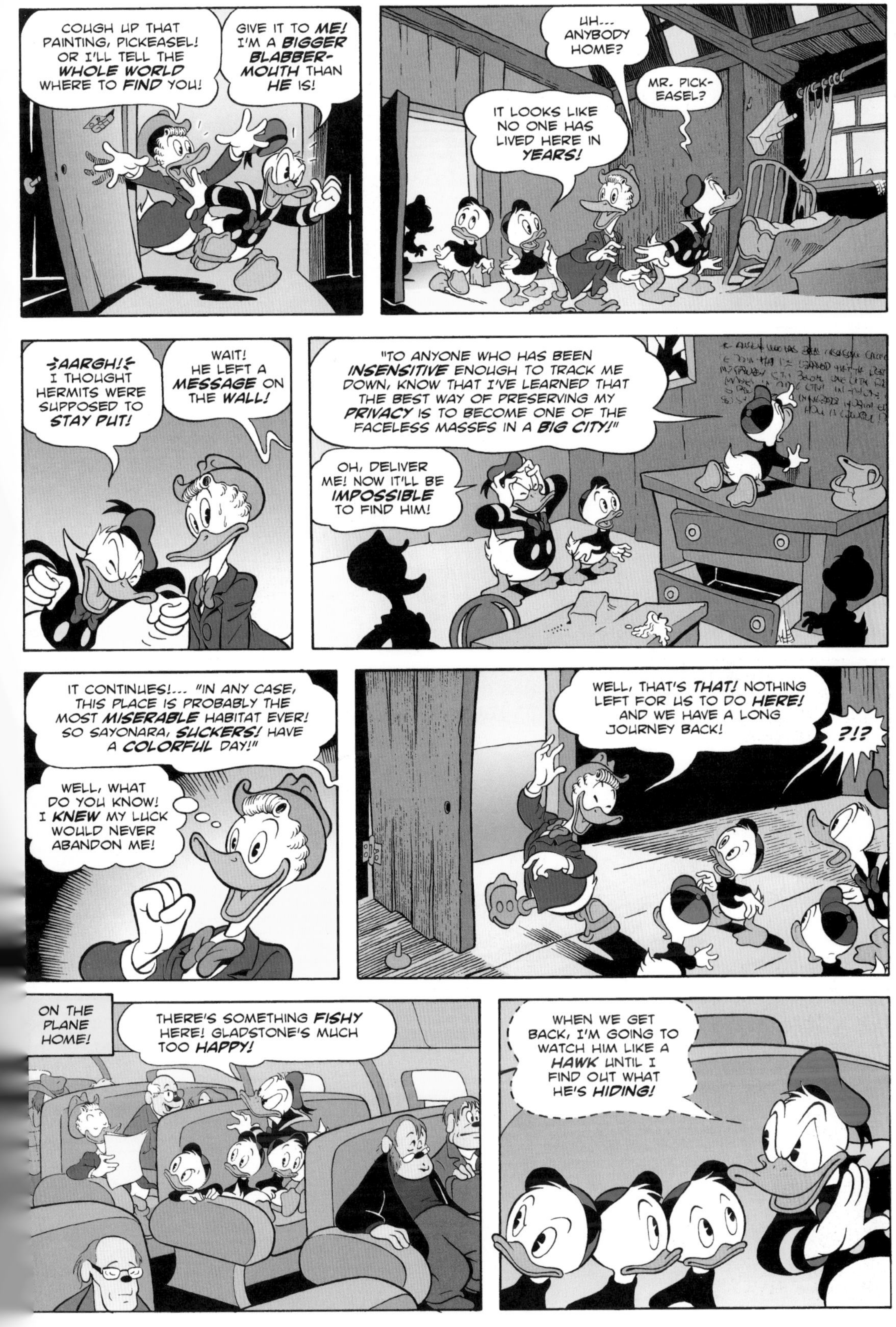
COUGH UP THAT PAINTING, PICKEASEL! OR I'LL TELL THE WHOLE WORLD WHERE TO FIND YOU!
GIVE IT TO ME! I'M A BIGGER BLABBER-MOUTH THAN HE IS!
UH... ANYBODY HOME?
MR. PICK-EASEL?
IT LOOKS LIKE NO ONE HAS LIVED HERE IN YEARS!
AARGH! I THOUGHT HERMITS WERE SUPPOSED TO STAY PUT!
WAIT! HE LEFT A MESSAGE ON THE WALL!
"TO ANYONE WHO HAS BEEN INSENSITIVE ENOUGH TO TRACK ME DOWN, KNOW THAT I'VE LEARNED THAT THE BEST WAY OF PRESERVING MY PRIVACY IS TO BECOME ONE OF THE FACELESS MASSES IN A BIG CITY!"
OH, DELIVER ME! NOW IT'LL BE IMPOSSIBLE TO FIND HIM!
IT CONTINUES!... "IN ANY CASE, THIS PLACE IS PROBABLY THE MOST MISERABLE HABITAT EVER! SO SAYONARA, SUCKERS! HAVE A COLORFUL DAY!"
WELL, WHAT DO YOU KNOW! I KNEW MY LUCK WOULD NEVER ABANDON ME!
WELL, THAT'S THAT! NOTHING LEFT FOR US TO DO HERE! AND WE HAVE A LONG JOURNEY BACK!
?!?
ON THE PLANE HOME!
THERE'S SOMETHING FISHY HERE! GLADSTONE'S MUCH TOO HAPPY!
WHEN WE GET BACK, I'M GOING TO WATCH HIM LIKE A HAWK UNTIL I FIND OUT WHAT HE'S HIDING!

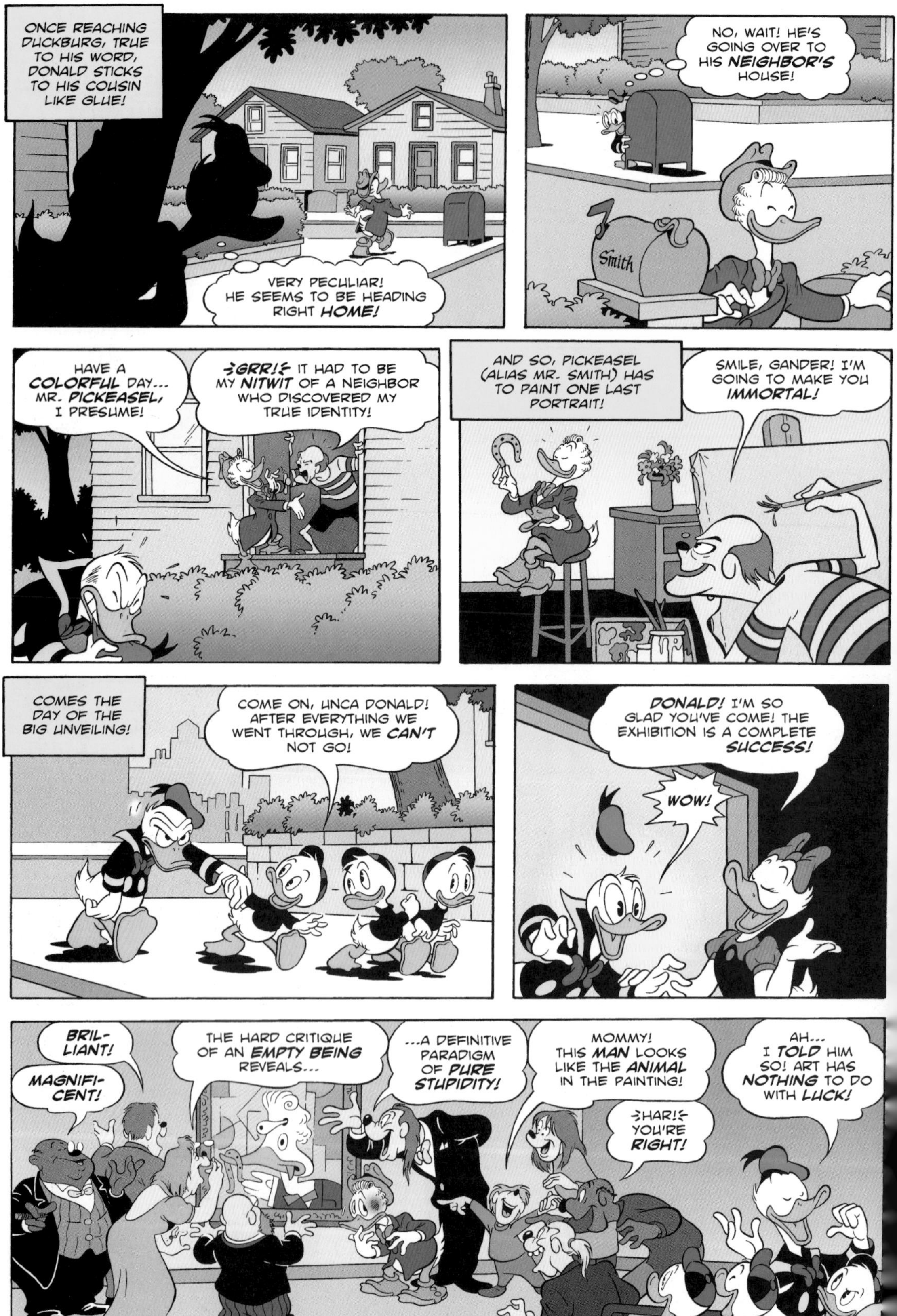

ONCE REACHING DUCKBURG, TRUE TO HIS WORD, DONALD STICKS TO HIS COUSIN LIKE GLUE!
VERY PECULIAR! HE SEEMS TO BE HEADING RIGHT HOME!
NO, WAIT! HE'S GOING OVER TO HIS NEIGHBOR'S HOUSE!
Smith
HAVE A COLORFUL DAY... MR. PICKEASEL, I PRESUME!
GRR! IT HAD TO BE MY NITWIT OF A NEIGHBOR WHO DISCOVERED MY TRUE IDENTITY!
AND SO, PICKEASEL (ALIAS MR. SMITH) HAS TO PAINT ONE LAST PORTRAIT!
SMILE, GANDER! I'M GOING TO MAKE YOU IMMORTAL!
COMES THE DAY OF THE BIG UNVEILING!
COME ON, UNCA DONALD! AFTER EVERYTHING WE WENT THROUGH, WE CAN'T NOT GO!
DONALD! I'M SO GLAD YOU'VE COME! THE EXHIBITION IS A COMPLETE SUCCESS!
WOW!
BRIL-LIANT!
MAGNIFI-CENT!
THE HARD CRITIQUE OF AN EMPTY BEING REVEALS...
...A DEFINITIVE PARADIGM OF PURE STUPIDITY!
MOMMY! THIS MAN LOOKS LIKE THE ANIMAL IN THE PAINTING!
HAR! YOU'RE RIGHT!
AH... I TOLD HIM SO! ART HAS NOTHING TO DO WITH LUCK!

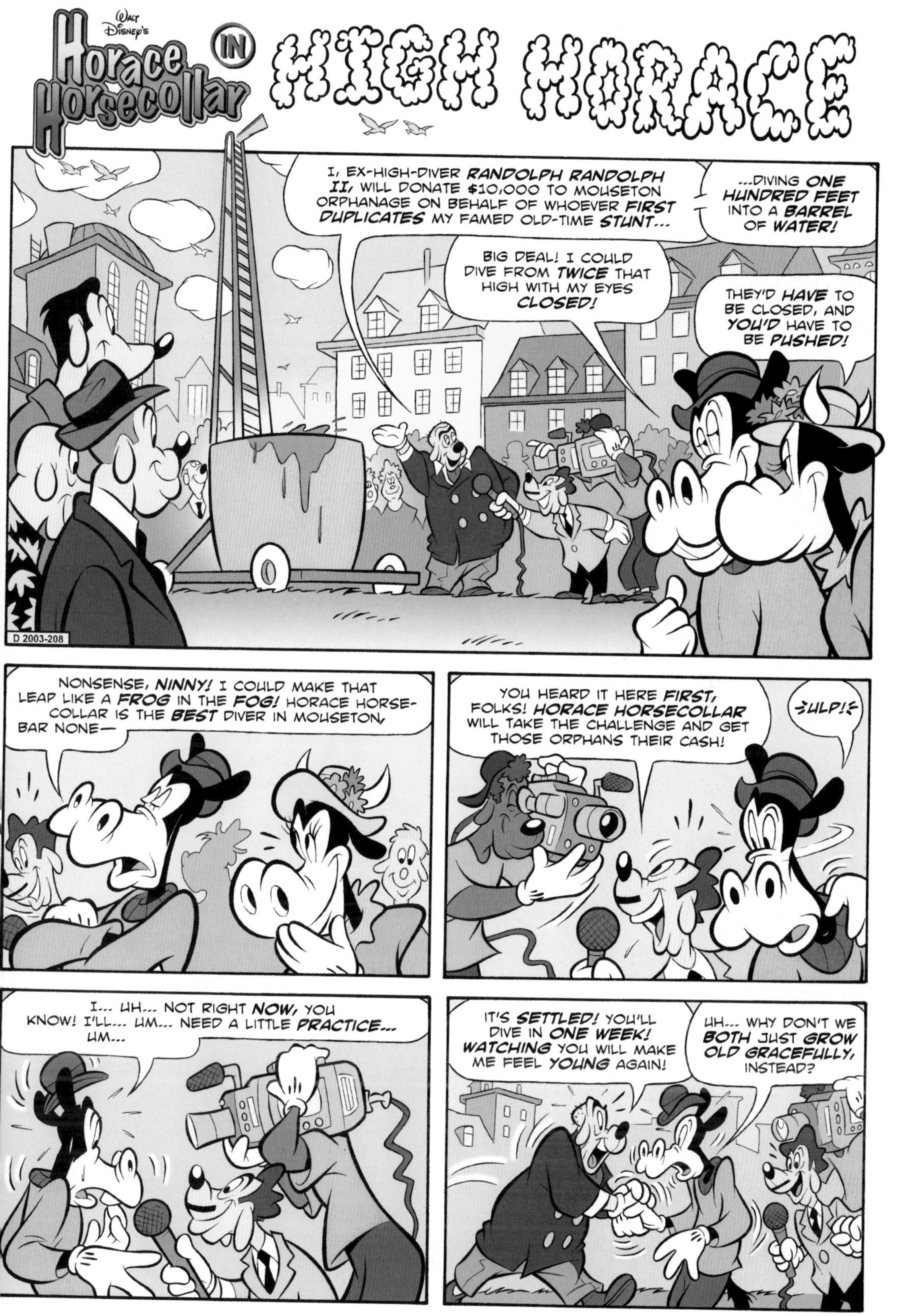
Walt Disney's
Horace Horsecollar
IN
HIGH HORACE
I, EX-HIGH-DIVER RANDOLPH RANDOLPH II, WILL DONATE $10,000 TO MOUSETON ORPHANAGE ON BEHALF OF WHOEVER FIRST DUPLICATES MY FAMED OLD-TIME STUNT...
...DIVING ONE HUNDRED FEET INTO A BARREL OF WATER!
BIG DEAL! I COULD DIVE FROM TWICE THAT HIGH WITH MY EYES CLOSED!
THEY'D HAVE TO BE CLOSED, AND YOU'D HAVE TO BE PUSHED!
D 2003-208
NONSENSE, NINNY! I COULD MAKE THAT LEAP LIKE A FROG IN THE FOG! HORACE HORSE-COLLAR IS THE BEST DIVER IN MOUSETON, BAR NONE—
YOU HEARD IT HERE FIRST, FOLKS! HORACE HORSECOLLAR WILL TAKE THE CHALLENGE AND GET THOSE ORPHANS THEIR CASH!
ULP!
I... UH... NOT RIGHT NOW, YOU KNOW! I'LL... UM... NEED A LITTLE PRACTICE... UM...
IT'S SETTLED! YOU'LL DIVE IN ONE WEEK! WATCHING YOU WILL MAKE ME FEEL YOUNG AGAIN!
UH... WHY DON'T WE BOTH JUST GROW OLD GRACEFULLY, INSTEAD?

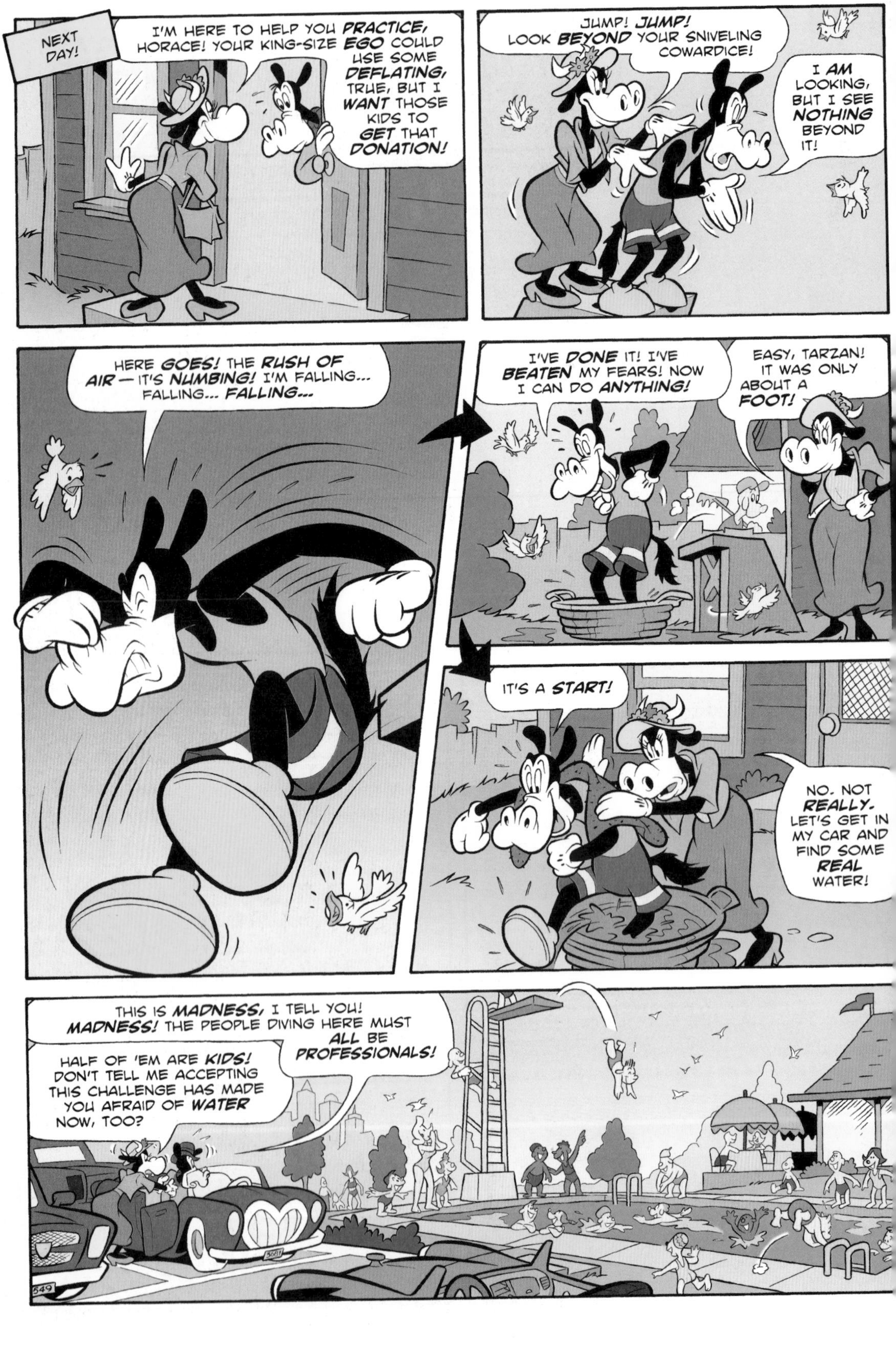
NEXT DAY!
I'M HERE TO HELP YOU PRACTICE, HORACE! YOUR KING-SIZE EGO COULD USE SOME DEFLATING, TRUE, BUT I WANT THOSE KIDS TO GET THAT DONATION!
JUMP! JUMP! LOOK BEYOND YOUR SNIVELING COWARDICE!
I AM LOOKING, BUT I SEE NOTHING BEYOND IT!
HERE GOES! THE RUSH OF AIR — IT'S NUMBING! I'M FALLING... FALLING... FALLING...
I'VE DONE IT! I'VE BEATEN MY FEARS! NOW I CAN DO ANYTHING!
EASY, TARZAN! IT WAS ONLY ABOUT A FOOT!
IT'S A START!
NO. NOT REALLY. LET'S GET IN MY CAR AND FIND SOME REAL WATER!
THIS IS MADNESS, I TELL YOU! MADNESS! THE PEOPLE DIVING HERE MUST ALL BE PROFESSIONALS!
HALF OF 'EM ARE KIDS! DON'T TELL ME ACCEPTING THIS CHALLENGE HAS MADE YOU AFRAID OF WATER NOW, TOO?

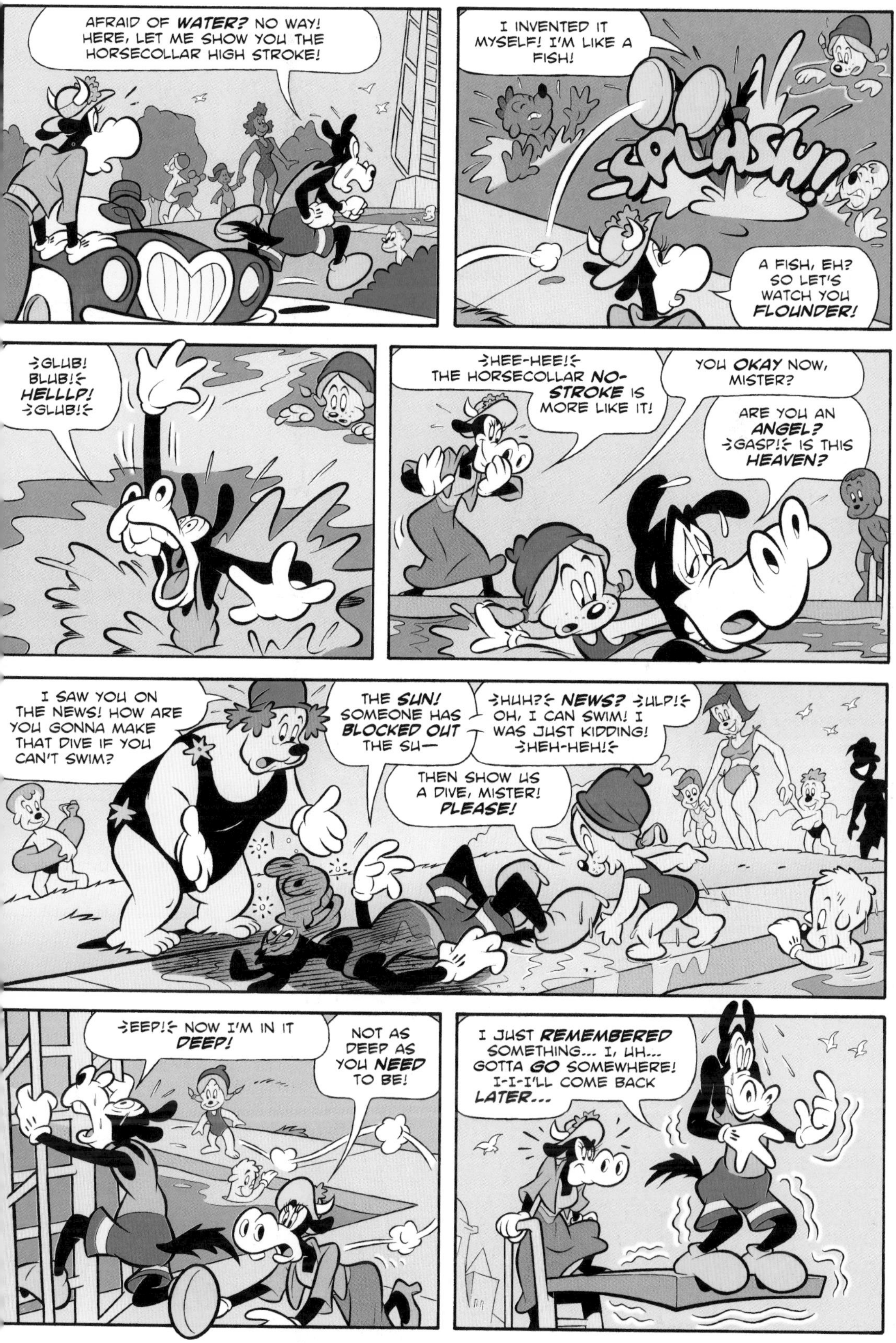

AFRAID OF WATER? NO WAY! HERE, LET ME SHOW YOU THE HORSECOLLAR HIGH STROKE!
I INVENTED IT MYSELF! I'M LIKE A FISH!
SPLASH!!
A FISH, EH? SO LET'S WATCH YOU FLOUNDER!
GLUB! BLUB! HELLLP! GLUB!
HEE-HEE! THE HORSECOLLAR NO-STROKE IS MORE LIKE IT!
YOU OKAY NOW, MISTER?
ARE YOU AN ANGEL? GASP! IS THIS HEAVEN?
I SAW YOU ON THE NEWS! HOW ARE YOU GONNA MAKE THAT DIVE IF YOU CAN'T SWIM?
THE SUN! SOMEONE HAS BLOCKED OUT THE SU—
HUH? NEWS? ULP! OH, I CAN SWIM! I WAS JUST KIDDING! HEH-HEH!
THEN SHOW US A DIVE, MISTER! PLEASE!
EEP! NOW I'M IN IT DEEP!
NOT AS DEEP AS YOU NEED TO BE!
I JUST REMEMBERED SOMETHING... I, UH... GOTTA GO SOMEWHERE! I-I-I'LL COME BACK LATER...

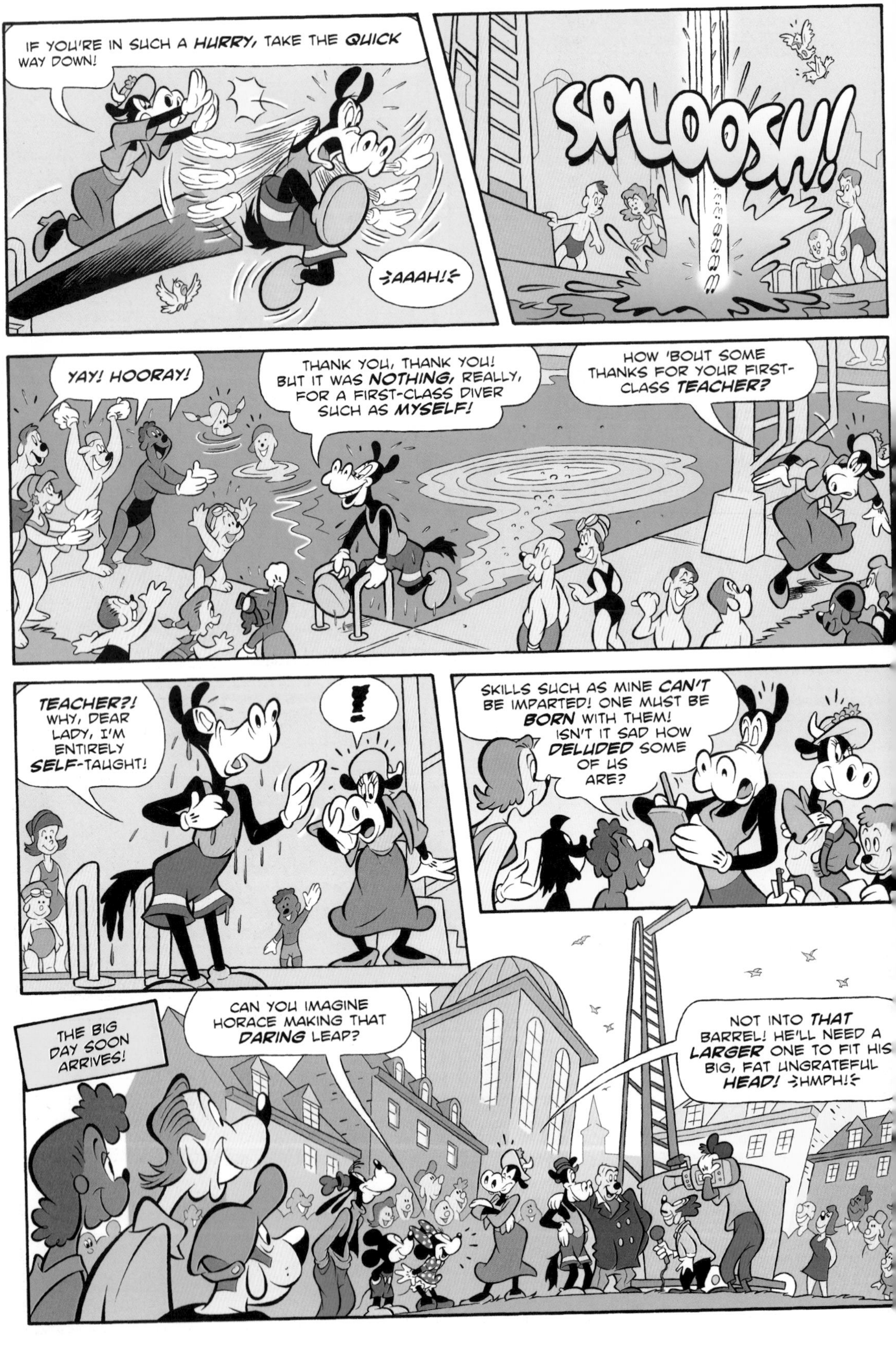
IF YOU'RE IN SUCH A HURRY, TAKE THE QUICK WAY DOWN!
AAAH!
SPLOOSH!
YAY! HOORAY!
THANK YOU, THANK YOU! BUT IT WAS NOTHING, REALLY, FOR A FIRST-CLASS DIVER SUCH AS MYSELF!
HOW 'BOUT SOME THANKS FOR YOUR FIRST-CLASS TEACHER?
TEACHER?! WHY, DEAR LADY, I'M ENTIRELY SELF-TAUGHT!
!
SKILLS SUCH AS MINE CAN'T BE IMPARTED! ONE MUST BE BORN WITH THEM! ISN'T IT SAD HOW DELUDED SOME OF US ARE?
THE BIG DAY SOON ARRIVES!
CAN YOU IMAGINE HORACE MAKING THAT DARING LEAP?
NOT INTO THAT BARREL! HE'LL NEED A LARGER ONE TO FIT HIS BIG, FAT UNGRATEFUL HEAD! HMPH!

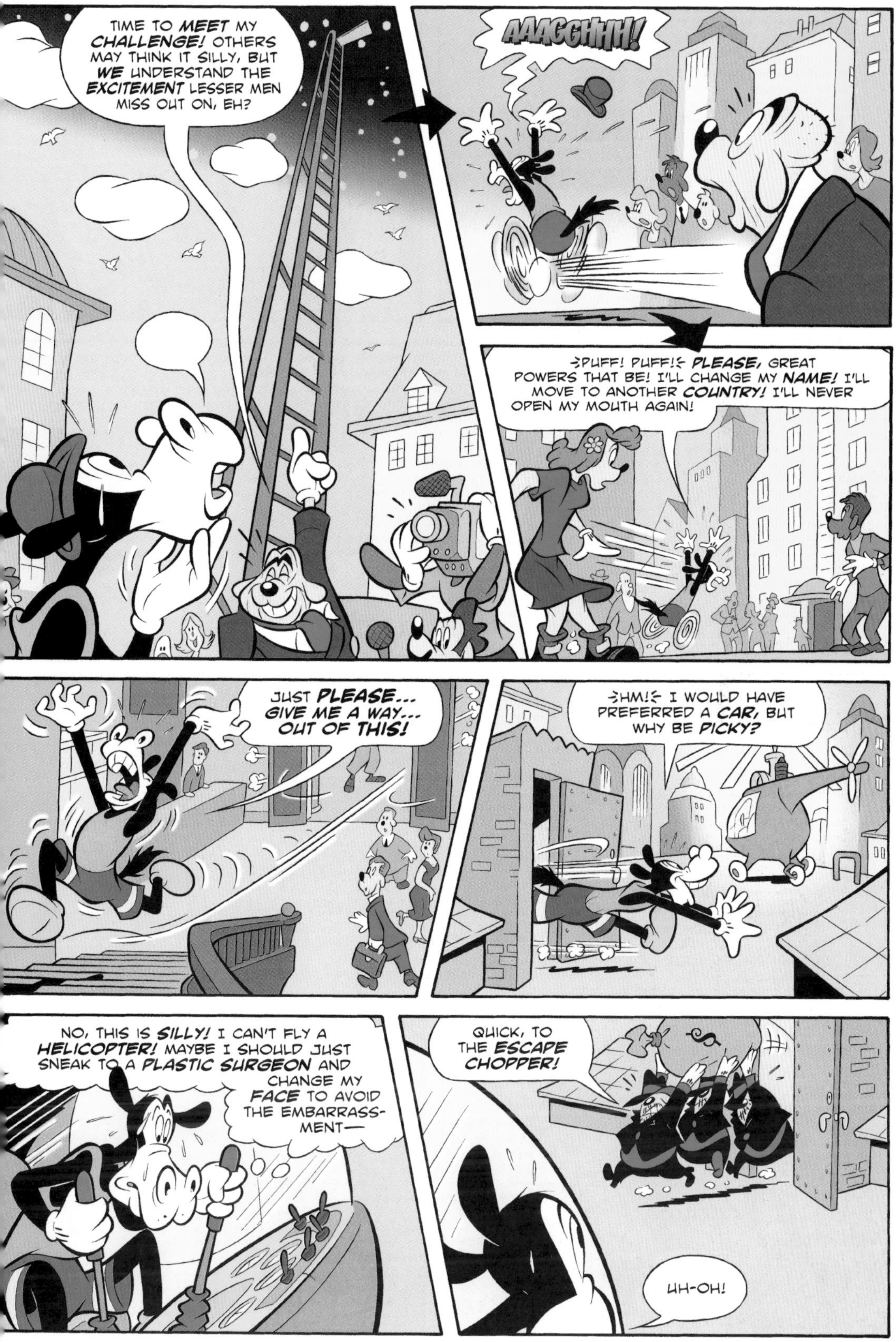
TIME TO MEET MY CHALLENGE! OTHERS MAY THINK IT SILLY, BUT WE UNDERSTAND THE EXCITEMENT LESSER MEN MISS OUT ON, EH?
AAAGGHHH!
-PUFF! PUFF!- PLEASE, GREAT POWERS THAT BE! I'LL CHANGE MY NAME! I'LL MOVE TO ANOTHER COUNTRY! I'LL NEVER OPEN MY MOUTH AGAIN!
JUST PLEASE... GIVE ME A WAY... OUT OF THIS!
-HM!- I WOULD HAVE PREFERRED A CAR, BUT WHY BE PICKY?
NO, THIS IS SILLY! I CAN'T FLY A HELICOPTER! MAYBE I SHOULD JUST SNEAK TO A PLASTIC SURGEON AND CHANGE MY FACE TO AVOID THE EMBARRASSMENT—
QUICK, TO THE ESCAPE CHOPPER!
UH-OH!

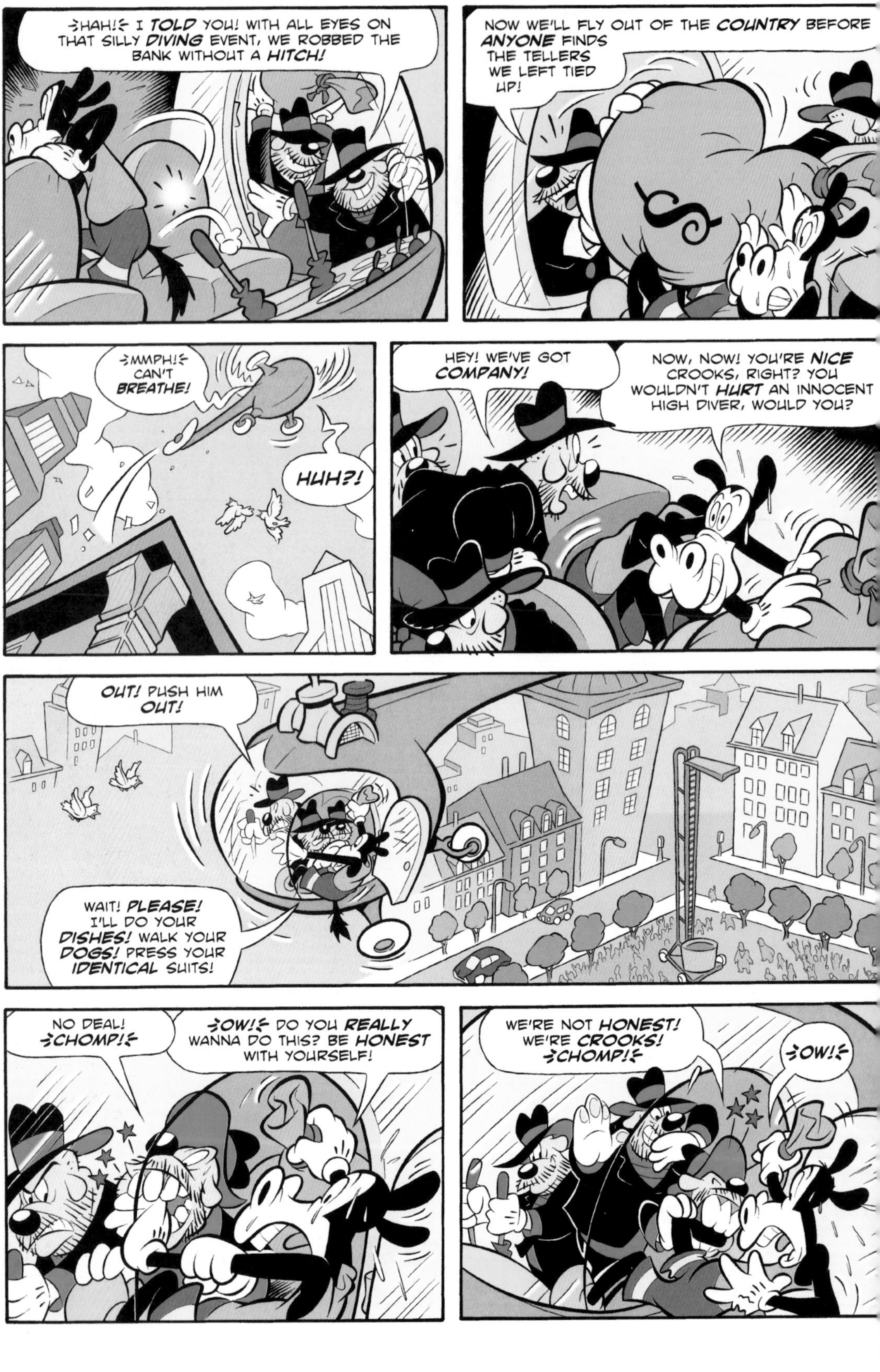

HAH! I TOLD YOU! WITH ALL EYES ON THAT SILLY DIVING EVENT, WE ROBBED THE BANK WITHOUT A HITCH!
NOW WE'LL FLY OUT OF THE COUNTRY BEFORE ANYONE FINDS THE TELLERS WE LEFT TIED UP!
MMPH! CAN'T BREATHE!
HUH?!
HEY! WE'VE GOT COMPANY!
NOW, NOW! YOU'RE NICE CROOKS, RIGHT? YOU WOULDN'T HURT AN INNOCENT HIGH DIVER, WOULD YOU?
OUT! PUSH HIM OUT!
WAIT! PLEASE! I'LL DO YOUR DISHES! WALK YOUR DOGS! PRESS YOUR IDENTICAL SUITS!
NO DEAL! CHOMP!
OW! DO YOU REALLY WANNA DO THIS? BE HONEST WITH YOURSELF!
WE'RE NOT HONEST! WE'RE CROOKS! CHOMP!
OW!

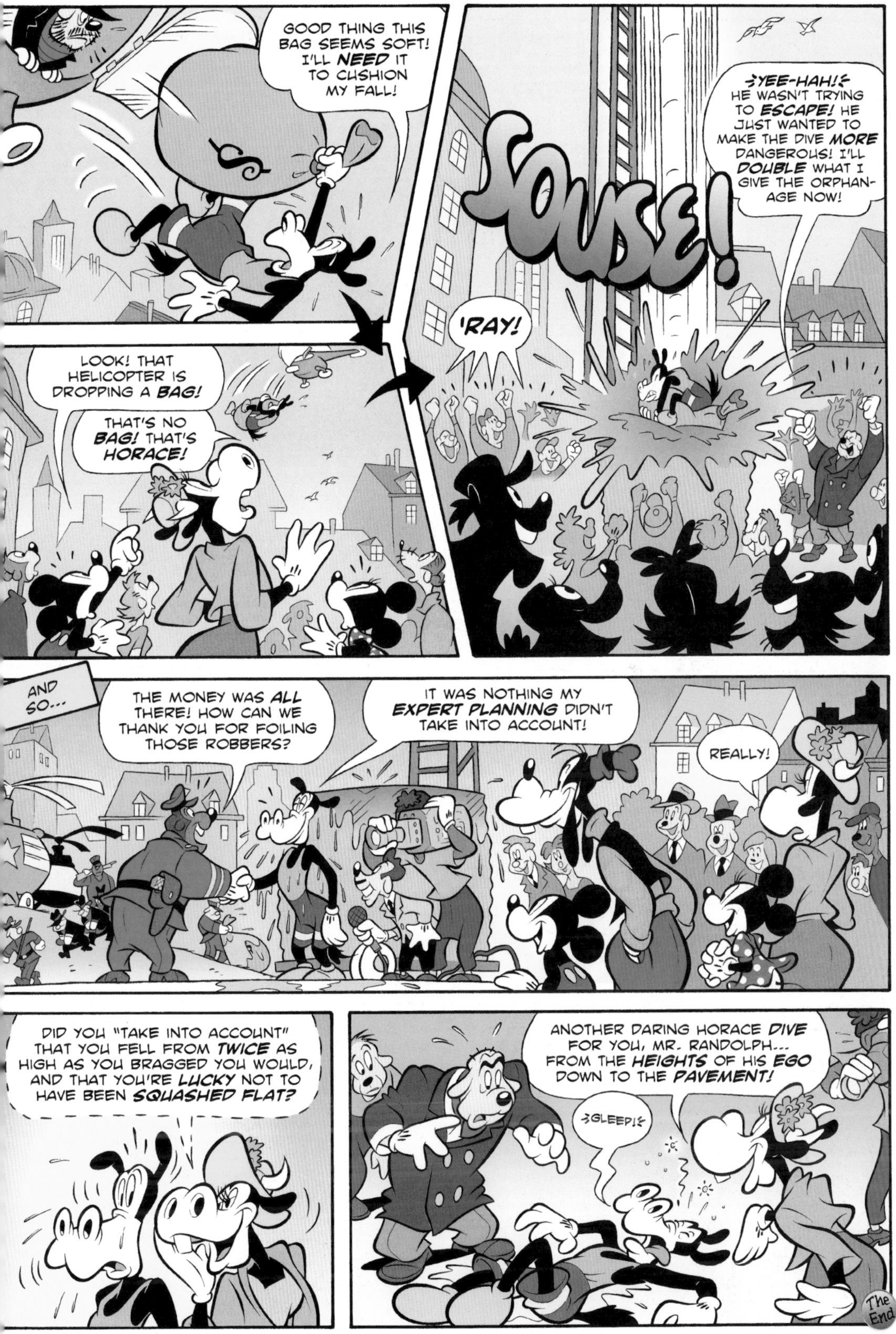
GOOD THING THIS BAG SEEMS SOFT! I'LL NEED IT TO CUSHION MY FALL!
LOOK! THAT HELICOPTER IS DROPPING A BAG!
THAT'S NO BAG! THAT'S HORACE!
SOUSE!
'RAY!
YEE-HAH! HE WASN'T TRYING TO ESCAPE! HE JUST WANTED TO MAKE THE DIVE MORE DANGEROUS! I'LL DOUBLE WHAT I GIVE THE ORPHAN-AGE NOW!
AND SO...
THE MONEY WAS ALL THERE! HOW CAN WE THANK YOU FOR FOILING THOSE ROBBERS?
IT WAS NOTHING MY EXPERT PLANNING DIDN'T TAKE INTO ACCOUNT!
REALLY!
DID YOU "TAKE INTO ACCOUNT" THAT YOU FELL FROM TWICE AS HIGH AS YOU BRAGGED YOU WOULD, AND THAT YOU'RE LUCKY NOT TO HAVE BEEN SQUASHED FLAT?
ANOTHER DARING HORACE DIVE FOR YOU, MR. RANDOLPH... FROM THE HEIGHTS OF HIS EGO DOWN TO THE PAVEMENT!
GLEEP!
The End

GET THE SKINNY ON MICKEY AND MINNIE

GEPPI'S
entertainment
MUSEUM

pop culture
with character

At Geppi's Entertainment Museum, you can visit the leader of the band that's made for you and me, not to mention his girlfriend and faithful pooch! Mickey, Minnie, Pluto and the rest of the Disney gang are on display at the museum, starting in the "When Heroes Unite" gallery. Mickey has evolved quite a bit over the years, and at GEM you'll see how changing styles and fashions played a role in making this mouse into the icon he is today.

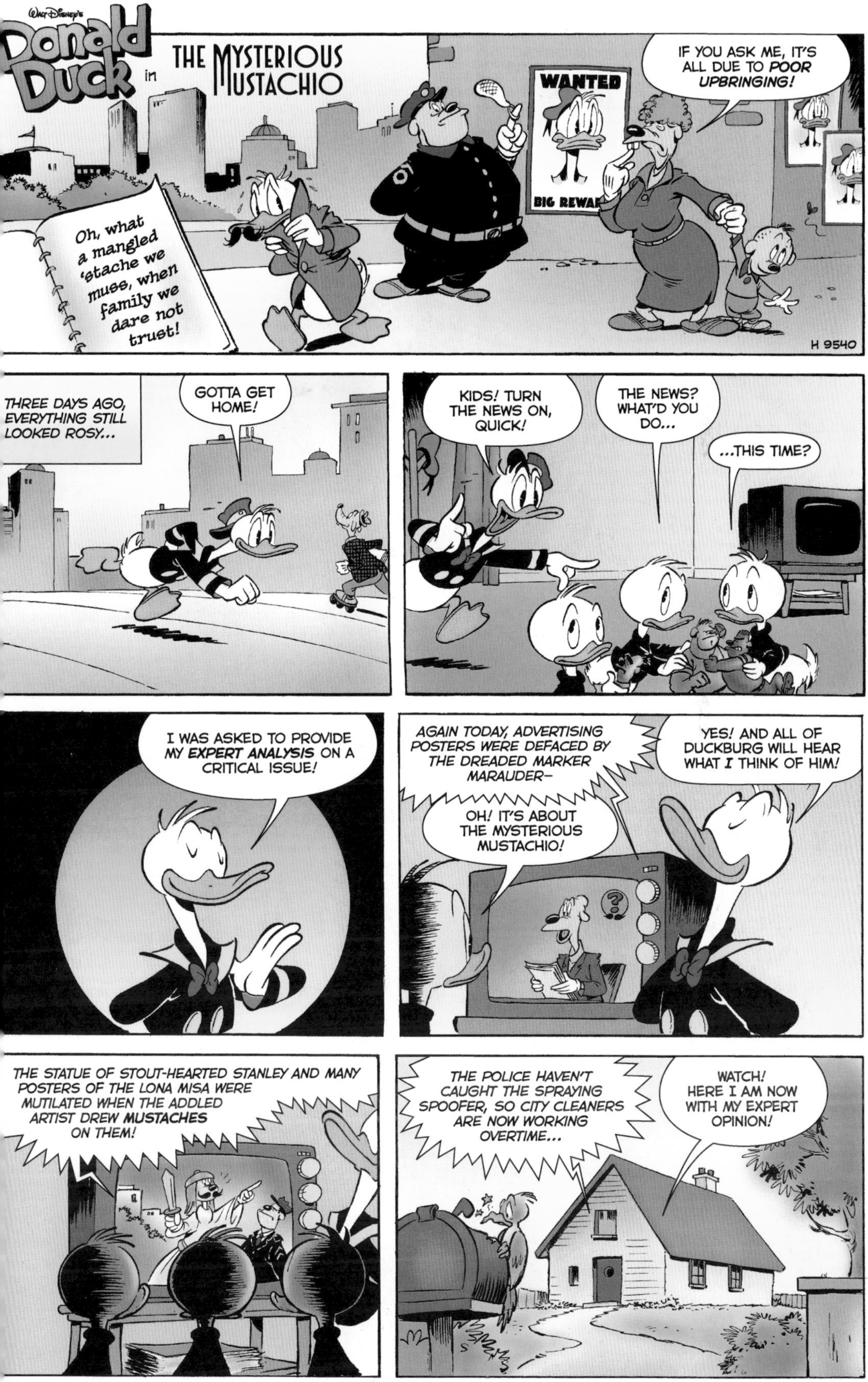
Walt Disney's
Donald Duck in
THE MYSTERIOUS MUSTACHIO
Oh, what a mangled 'stache we muss, when family we dare not trust!
WANTED
BIG REWA
IF YOU ASK ME, IT'S ALL DUE TO POOR UPBRINGING!
H 9540
THREE DAYS AGO, EVERYTHING STILL LOOKED ROSY...
GOTTA GET HOME!
KIDS! TURN THE NEWS ON, QUICK!
THE NEWS? WHAT'D YOU DO...
...THIS TIME?
I WAS ASKED TO PROVIDE MY EXPERT ANALYSIS ON A CRITICAL ISSUE!
AGAIN TODAY, ADVERTISING POSTERS WERE DEFACED BY THE DREADED MARKER MARAUDER–
YES! AND ALL OF DUCKBURG WILL HEAR WHAT I THINK OF HIM!
OH! IT'S ABOUT THE MYSTERIOUS MUSTACHIO!
THE STATUE OF STOUT-HEARTED STANLEY AND MANY POSTERS OF THE LONA MISA WERE MUTILATED WHEN THE ADDLED ARTIST DREW MUSTACHES ON THEM!
THE POLICE HAVEN'T CAUGHT THE SPRAYING SPOOFER, SO CITY CLEANERS ARE NOW WORKING OVERTIME...
WATCH! HERE I AM NOW WITH MY EXPERT OPINION!

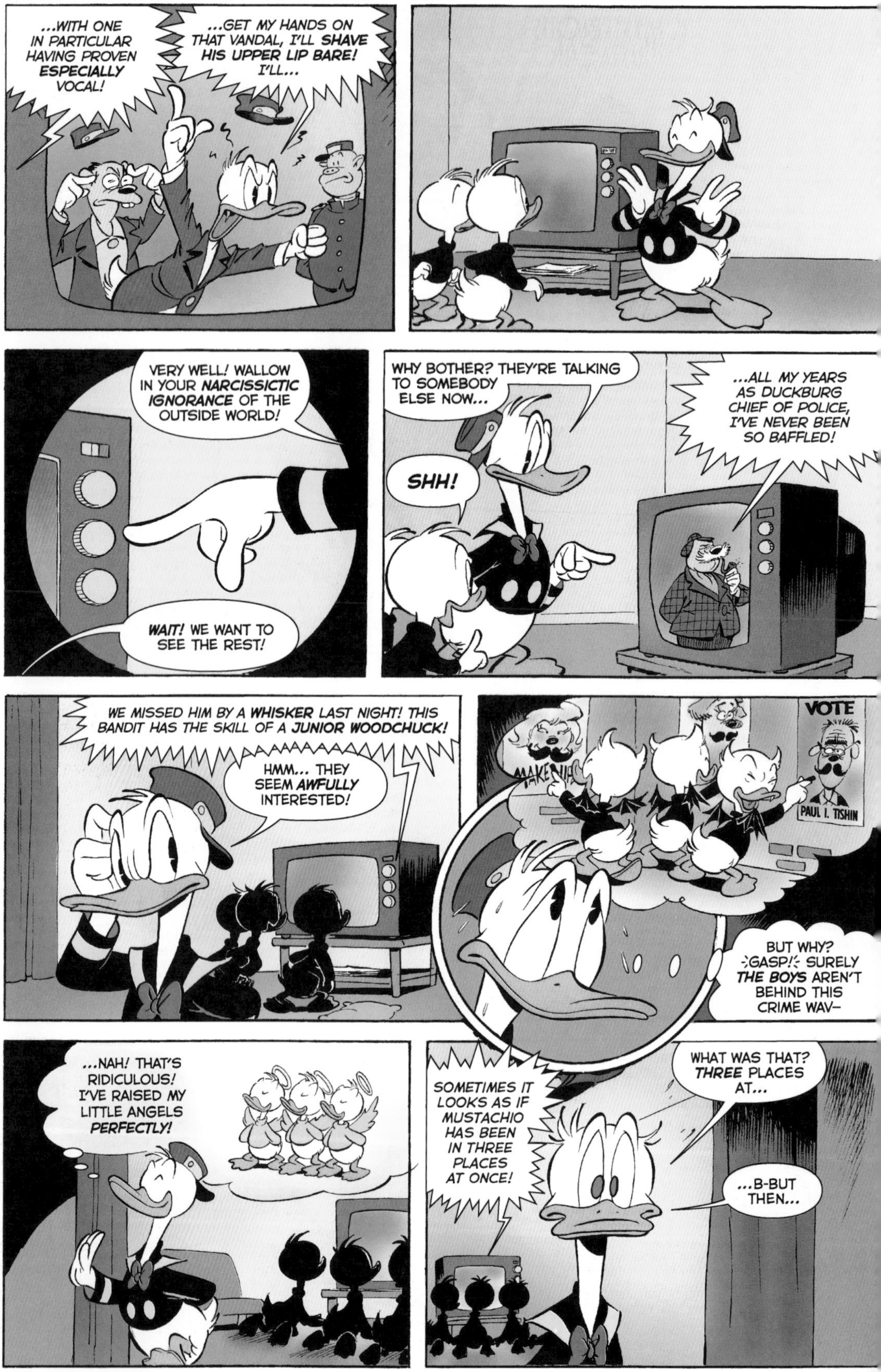
...WITH ONE IN PARTICULAR HAVING PROVEN **ESPECIALLY** VOCAL!
...GET MY HANDS ON THAT VANDAL, I'LL **SHAVE HIS UPPER LIP BARE!** I'LL...
VERY WELL! WALLOW IN YOUR **NARCISSICTIC IGNORANCE** OF THE OUTSIDE WORLD!
WAIT! WE WANT TO SEE THE REST!
WHY BOTHER? THEY'RE TALKING TO SOMEBODY ELSE NOW...
SHH!
...ALL MY YEARS AS DUCKBURG CHIEF OF POLICE, I'VE NEVER BEEN SO BAFFLED!
WE MISSED HIM BY A **WHISKER** LAST NIGHT! THIS BANDIT HAS THE SKILL OF A **JUNIOR WOODCHUCK!**
HMM... THEY SEEM **AWFULLY** INTERESTED!
VOTE
PAUL I. TISHIN
BUT WHY? ⁝GASP!⁝ SURELY **THE BOYS** AREN'T BEHIND THIS CRIME WAV–
...NAH! THAT'S RIDICULOUS! I'VE RAISED MY LITTLE ANGELS **PERFECTLY!**
SOMETIMES IT LOOKS AS IF MUSTACHIO HAS BEEN IN THREE PLACES AT ONCE!
WHAT WAS THAT? **THREE** PLACES AT...
...B-BUT THEN...

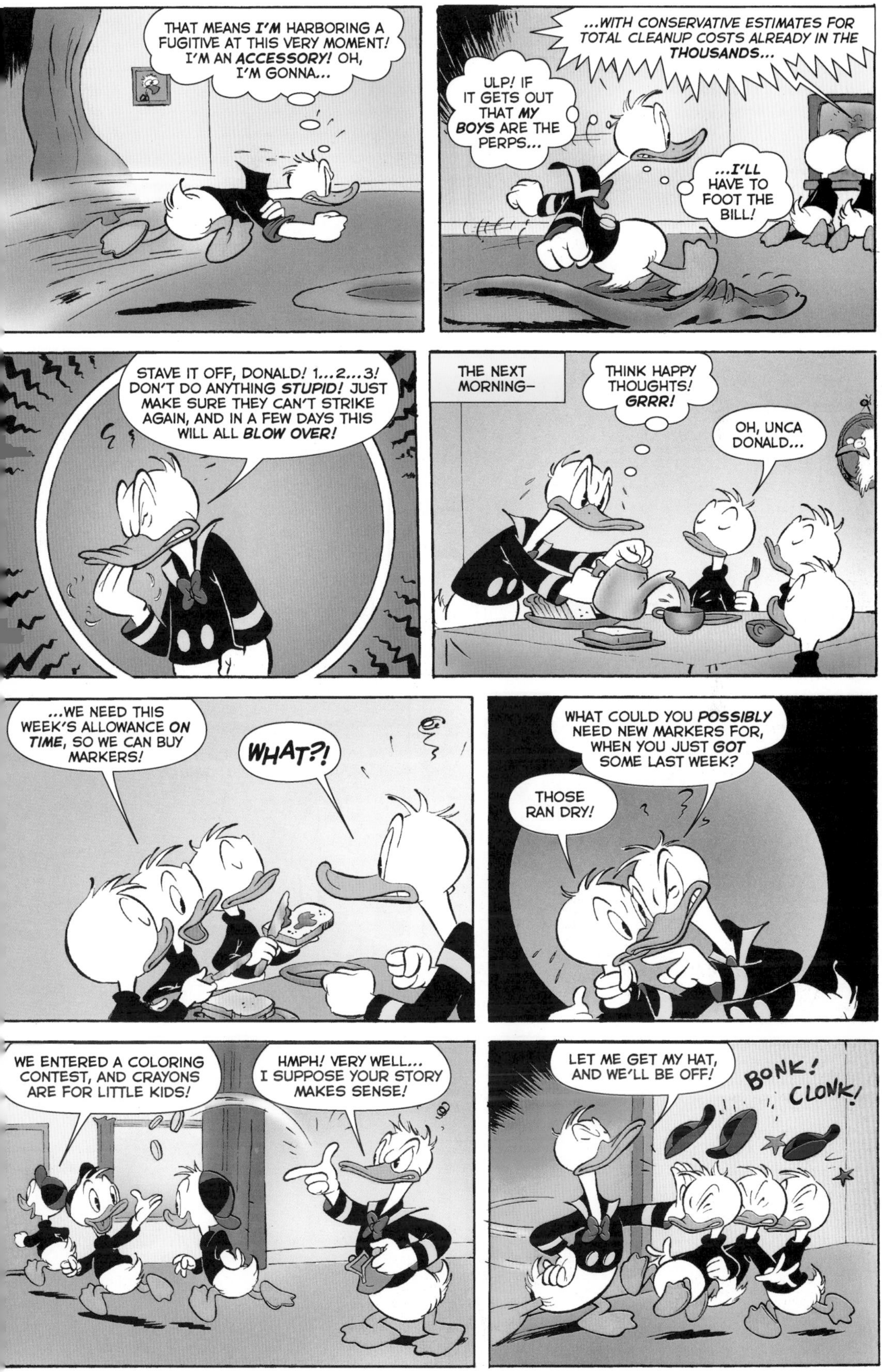
THAT MEANS I'M HARBORING A FUGITIVE AT THIS VERY MOMENT! I'M AN ACCESSORY! OH, I'M GONNA...
...WITH CONSERVATIVE ESTIMATES FOR TOTAL CLEANUP COSTS ALREADY IN THE THOUSANDS...
ULP! IF IT GETS OUT THAT MY BOYS ARE THE PERPS...
...I'LL HAVE TO FOOT THE BILL!
STAVE IT OFF, DONALD! 1...2...3! DON'T DO ANYTHING STUPID! JUST MAKE SURE THEY CAN'T STRIKE AGAIN, AND IN A FEW DAYS THIS WILL ALL BLOW OVER!
THE NEXT MORNING–
THINK HAPPY THOUGHTS! GRRR!
OH, UNCA DONALD...
...WE NEED THIS WEEK'S ALLOWANCE ON TIME, SO WE CAN BUY MARKERS!
WHAT?!
WHAT COULD YOU POSSIBLY NEED NEW MARKERS FOR, WHEN YOU JUST GOT SOME LAST WEEK?
THOSE RAN DRY!
WE ENTERED A COLORING CONTEST, AND CRAYONS ARE FOR LITTLE KIDS!
HMPH! VERY WELL... I SUPPOSE YOUR STORY MAKES SENSE!
LET ME GET MY HAT, AND WE'LL BE OFF!
BONK! CLONK!

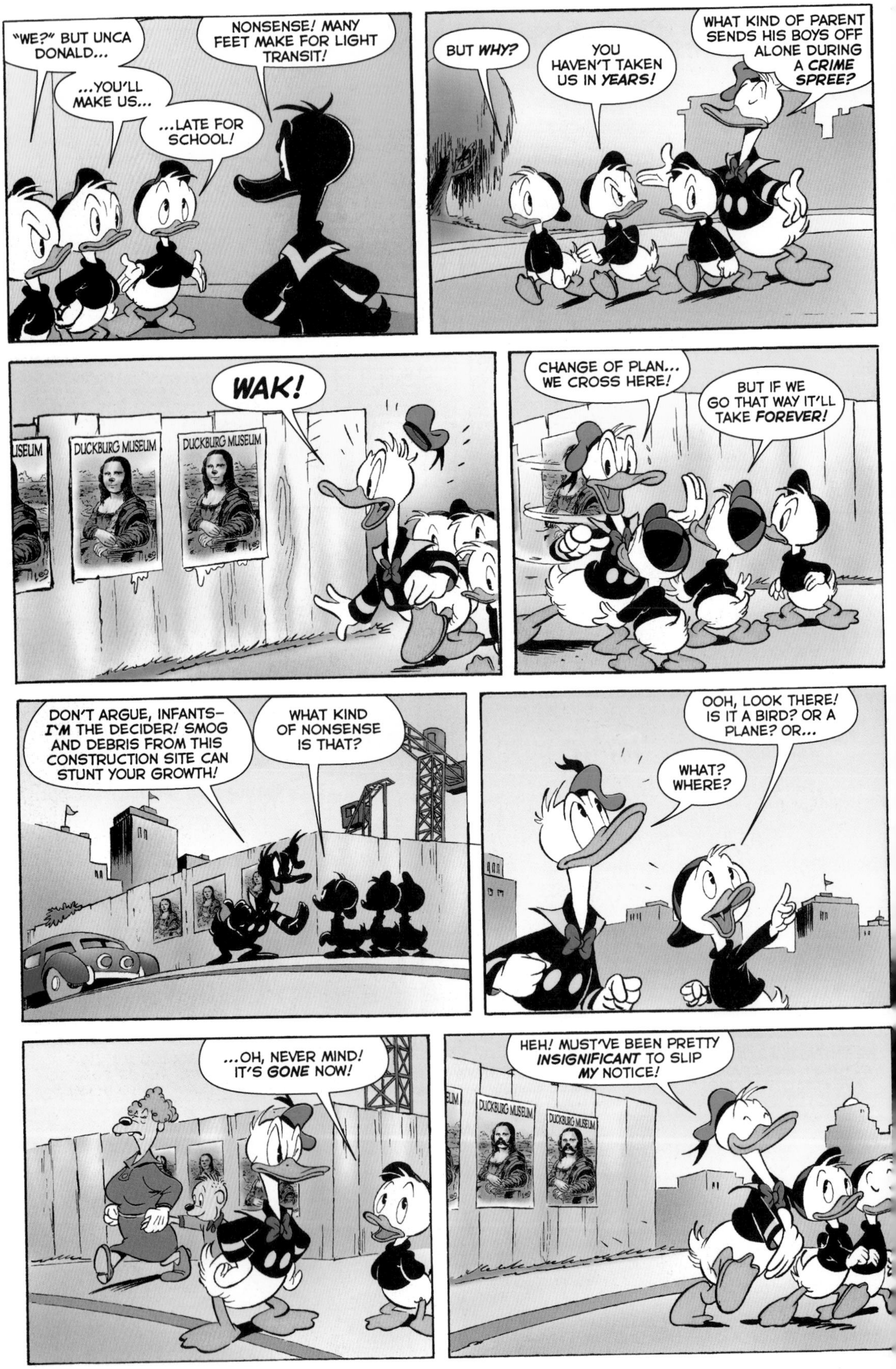
"WE?" BUT UNCA DONALD...
...YOU'LL MAKE US...
...LATE FOR SCHOOL!
NONSENSE! MANY FEET MAKE FOR LIGHT TRANSIT!
BUT WHY?
YOU HAVEN'T TAKEN US IN YEARS!
WHAT KIND OF PARENT SENDS HIS BOYS OFF ALONE DURING A CRIME SPREE?
WAK!
DUCKBURG MUSEUM
DUCKBURG MUSEUM
CHANGE OF PLAN... WE CROSS HERE!
BUT IF WE GO THAT WAY IT'LL TAKE FOREVER!
DON'T ARGUE, INFANTS— I'M THE DECIDER! SMOG AND DEBRIS FROM THIS CONSTRUCTION SITE CAN STUNT YOUR GROWTH!
WHAT KIND OF NONSENSE IS THAT?
OOH, LOOK THERE! IS IT A BIRD? OR A PLANE? OR...
WHAT? WHERE?
...OH, NEVER MIND! IT'S GONE NOW!
HEH! MUST'VE BEEN PRETTY INSIGNIFICANT TO SLIP MY NOTICE!
DUCKBURG MUSEUM
DUCKBURG MUSEUM

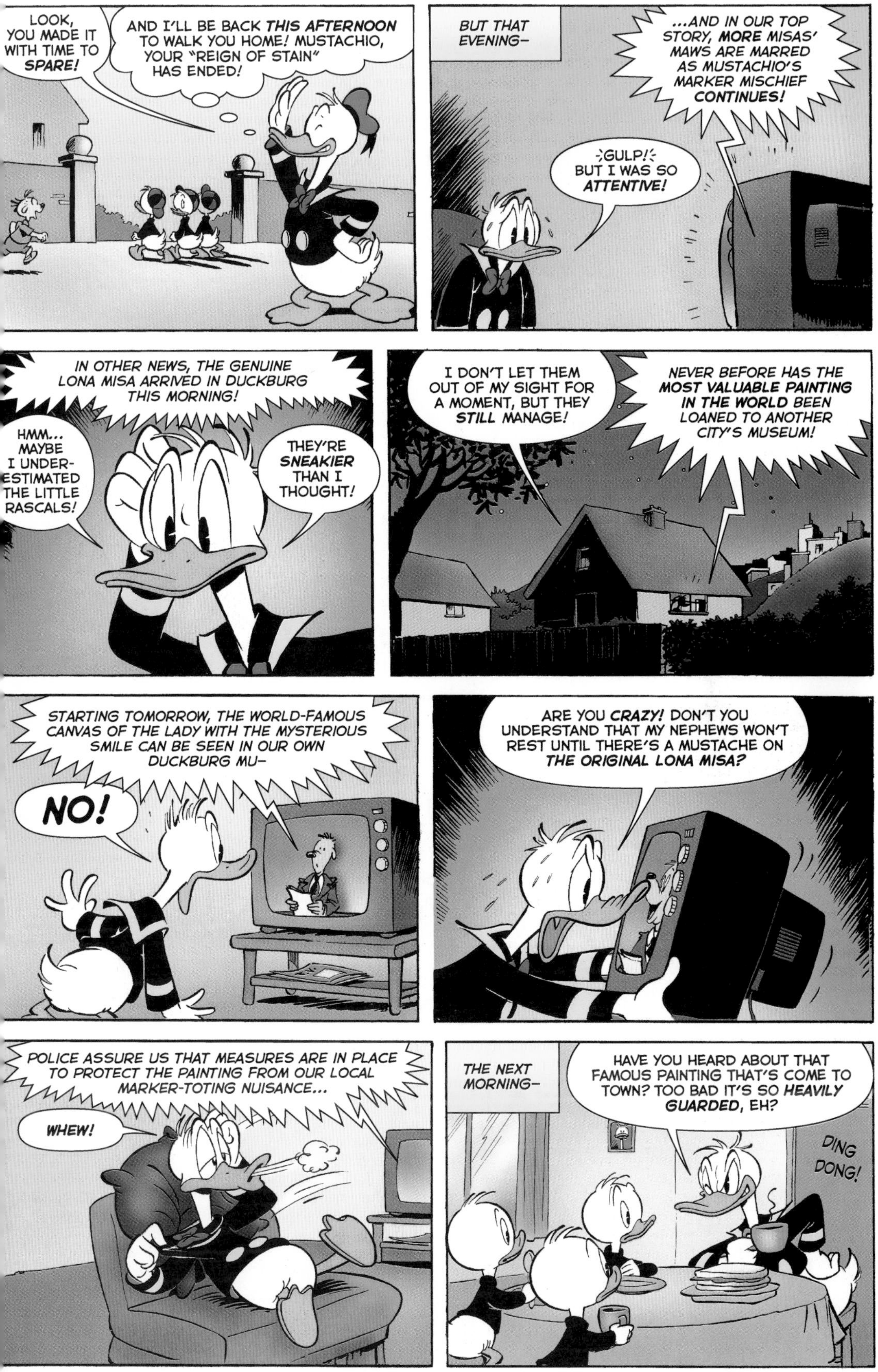

LOOK, YOU MADE IT WITH TIME TO SPARE!
AND I'LL BE BACK THIS AFTERNOON TO WALK YOU HOME! MUSTACHIO, YOUR "REIGN OF STAIN" HAS ENDED!
BUT THAT EVENING–
...AND IN OUR TOP STORY, MORE MISAS' MAWS ARE MARRED AS MUSTACHIO'S MARKER MISCHIEF CONTINUES!
GULP! BUT I WAS SO ATTENTIVE!
IN OTHER NEWS, THE GENUINE LONA MISA ARRIVED IN DUCKBURG THIS MORNING!
HMM... MAYBE I UNDER-ESTIMATED THE LITTLE RASCALS!
THEY'RE SNEAKIER THAN I THOUGHT!
I DON'T LET THEM OUT OF MY SIGHT FOR A MOMENT, BUT THEY STILL MANAGE!
NEVER BEFORE HAS THE MOST VALUABLE PAINTING IN THE WORLD BEEN LOANED TO ANOTHER CITY'S MUSEUM!
STARTING TOMORROW, THE WORLD-FAMOUS CANVAS OF THE LADY WITH THE MYSTERIOUS SMILE CAN BE SEEN IN OUR OWN DUCKBURG MU–
NO!
ARE YOU CRAZY! DON'T YOU UNDERSTAND THAT MY NEPHEWS WON'T REST UNTIL THERE'S A MUSTACHE ON THE ORIGINAL LONA MISA?
POLICE ASSURE US THAT MEASURES ARE IN PLACE TO PROTECT THE PAINTING FROM OUR LOCAL MARKER-TOTING NUISANCE...
WHEW!
THE NEXT MORNING–
HAVE YOU HEARD ABOUT THAT FAMOUS PAINTING THAT'S COME TO TOWN? TOO BAD IT'S SO HEAVILY GUARDED, EH?
DING DONG!

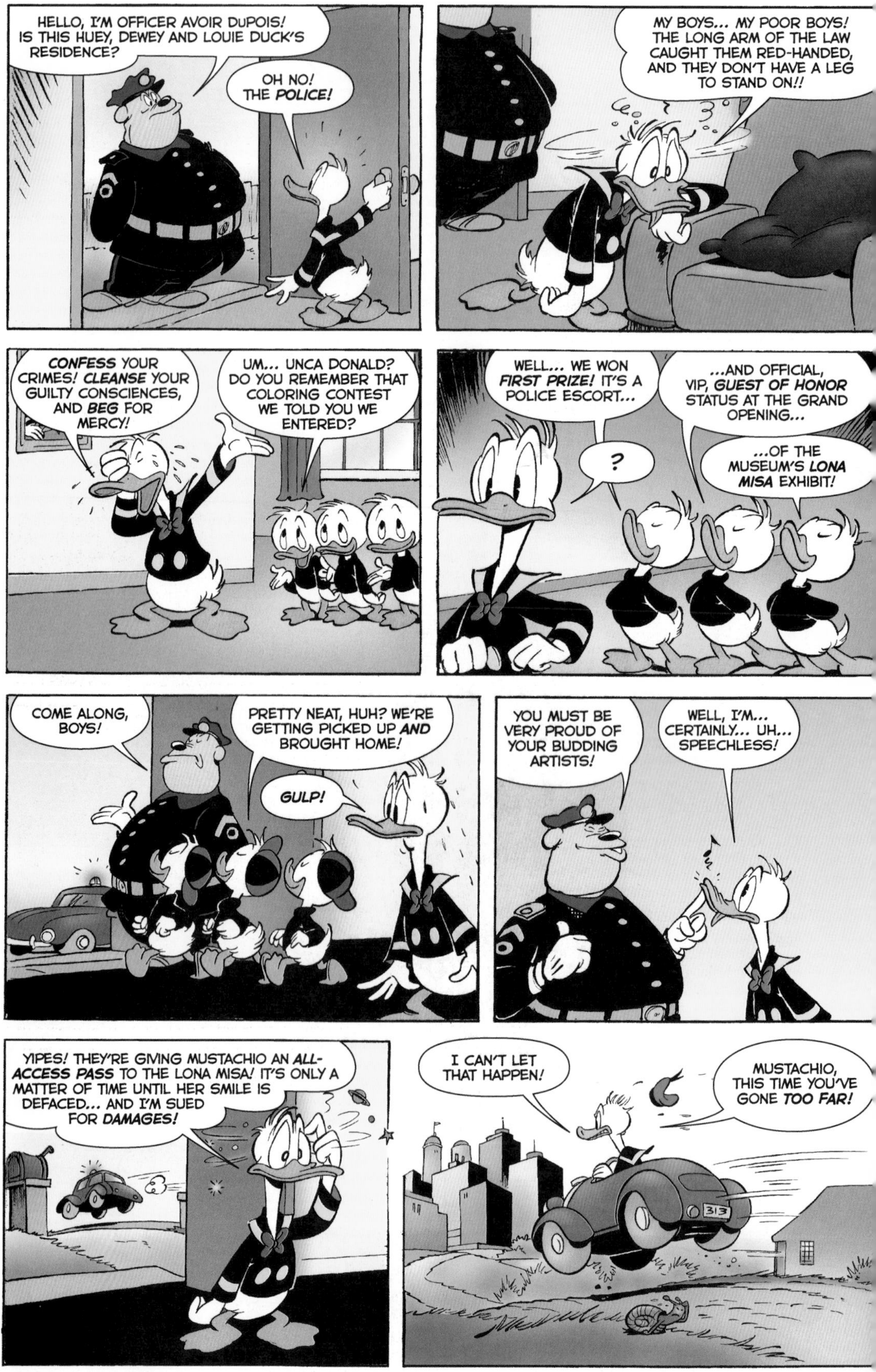
HELLO, I'M OFFICER AVOIR DUPOIS! IS THIS HUEY, DEWEY AND LOUIE DUCK'S RESIDENCE?
OH NO! THE POLICE!
MY BOYS... MY POOR BOYS! THE LONG ARM OF THE LAW CAUGHT THEM RED-HANDED, AND THEY DON'T HAVE A LEG TO STAND ON!!
CONFESS YOUR CRIMES! CLEANSE YOUR GUILTY CONSCIENCES, AND BEG FOR MERCY!
UM... UNCA DONALD? DO YOU REMEMBER THAT COLORING CONTEST WE TOLD YOU WE ENTERED?
WELL... WE WON FIRST PRIZE! IT'S A POLICE ESCORT...
?
...AND OFFICIAL, VIP, GUEST OF HONOR STATUS AT THE GRAND OPENING...
...OF THE MUSEUM'S LONA MISA EXHIBIT!
COME ALONG, BOYS!
PRETTY NEAT, HUH? WE'RE GETTING PICKED UP AND BROUGHT HOME!
GULP!
YOU MUST BE VERY PROUD OF YOUR BUDDING ARTISTS!
WELL, I'M... CERTAINLY... UH... SPEECHLESS!
YIPES! THEY'RE GIVING MUSTACHIO AN ALL-ACCESS PASS TO THE LONA MISA! IT'S ONLY A MATTER OF TIME UNTIL HER SMILE IS DEFACED... AND I'M SUED FOR DAMAGES!
I CAN'T LET THAT HAPPEN!
MUSTACHIO, THIS TIME YOU'VE GONE TOO FAR!
313

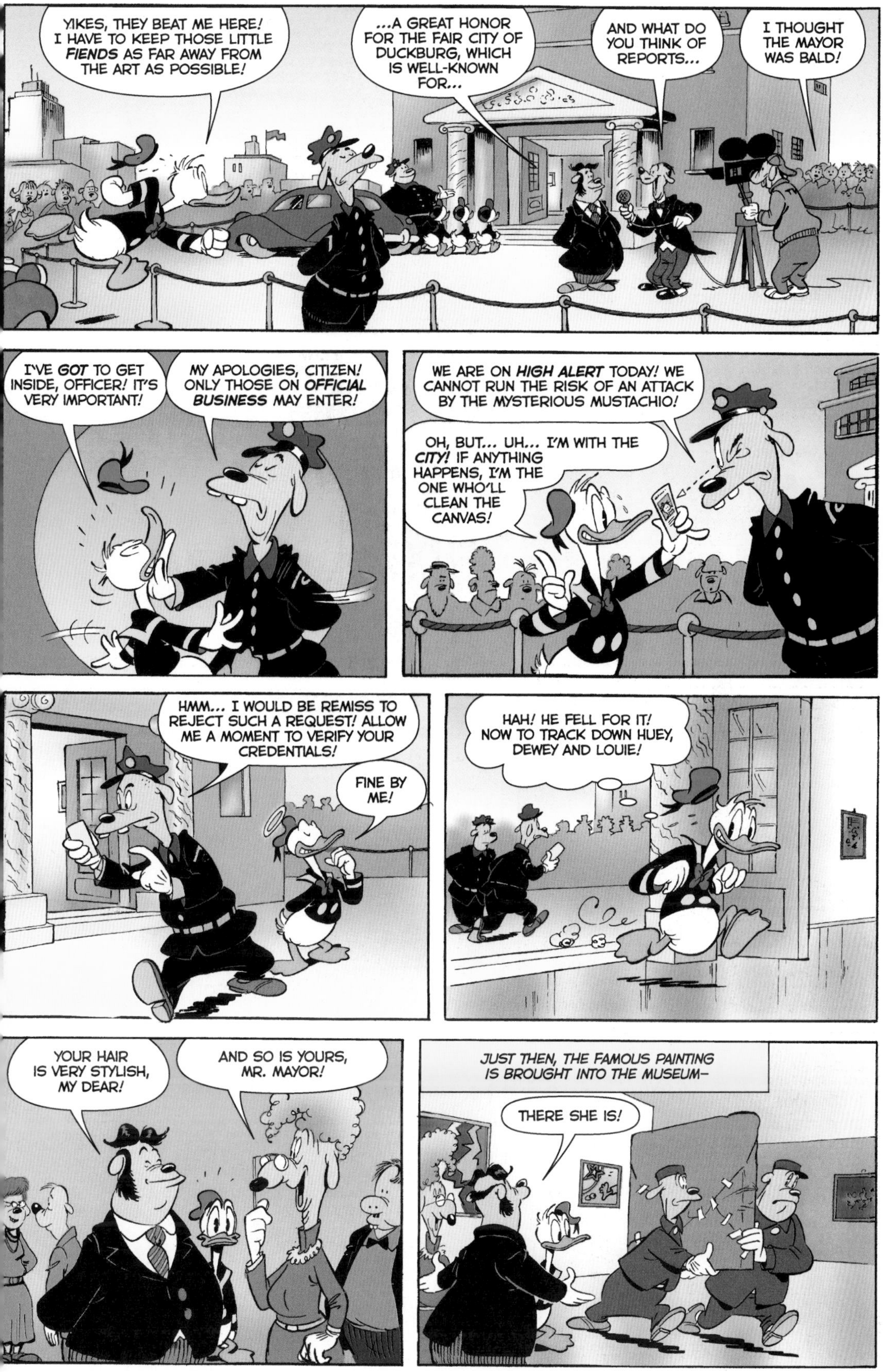
YIKES, THEY BEAT ME HERE! I HAVE TO KEEP THOSE LITTLE FIENDS AS FAR AWAY FROM THE ART AS POSSIBLE!
...A GREAT HONOR FOR THE FAIR CITY OF DUCKBURG, WHICH IS WELL-KNOWN FOR...
AND WHAT DO YOU THINK OF REPORTS...
I THOUGHT THE MAYOR WAS BALD!
I'VE GOT TO GET INSIDE, OFFICER! IT'S VERY IMPORTANT!
MY APOLOGIES, CITIZEN! ONLY THOSE ON OFFICIAL BUSINESS MAY ENTER!
WE ARE ON HIGH ALERT TODAY! WE CANNOT RUN THE RISK OF AN ATTACK BY THE MYSTERIOUS MUSTACHIO!
OH, BUT... UH... I'M WITH THE CITY! IF ANYTHING HAPPENS, I'M THE ONE WHO'LL CLEAN THE CANVAS!
HMM... I WOULD BE REMISS TO REJECT SUCH A REQUEST! ALLOW ME A MOMENT TO VERIFY YOUR CREDENTIALS!
FINE BY ME!
HAH! HE FELL FOR IT! NOW TO TRACK DOWN HUEY, DEWEY AND LOUIE!
YOUR HAIR IS VERY STYLISH, MY DEAR!
AND SO IS YOURS, MR. MAYOR!
JUST THEN, THE FAMOUS PAINTING IS BROUGHT INTO THE MUSEUM—
THERE SHE IS!

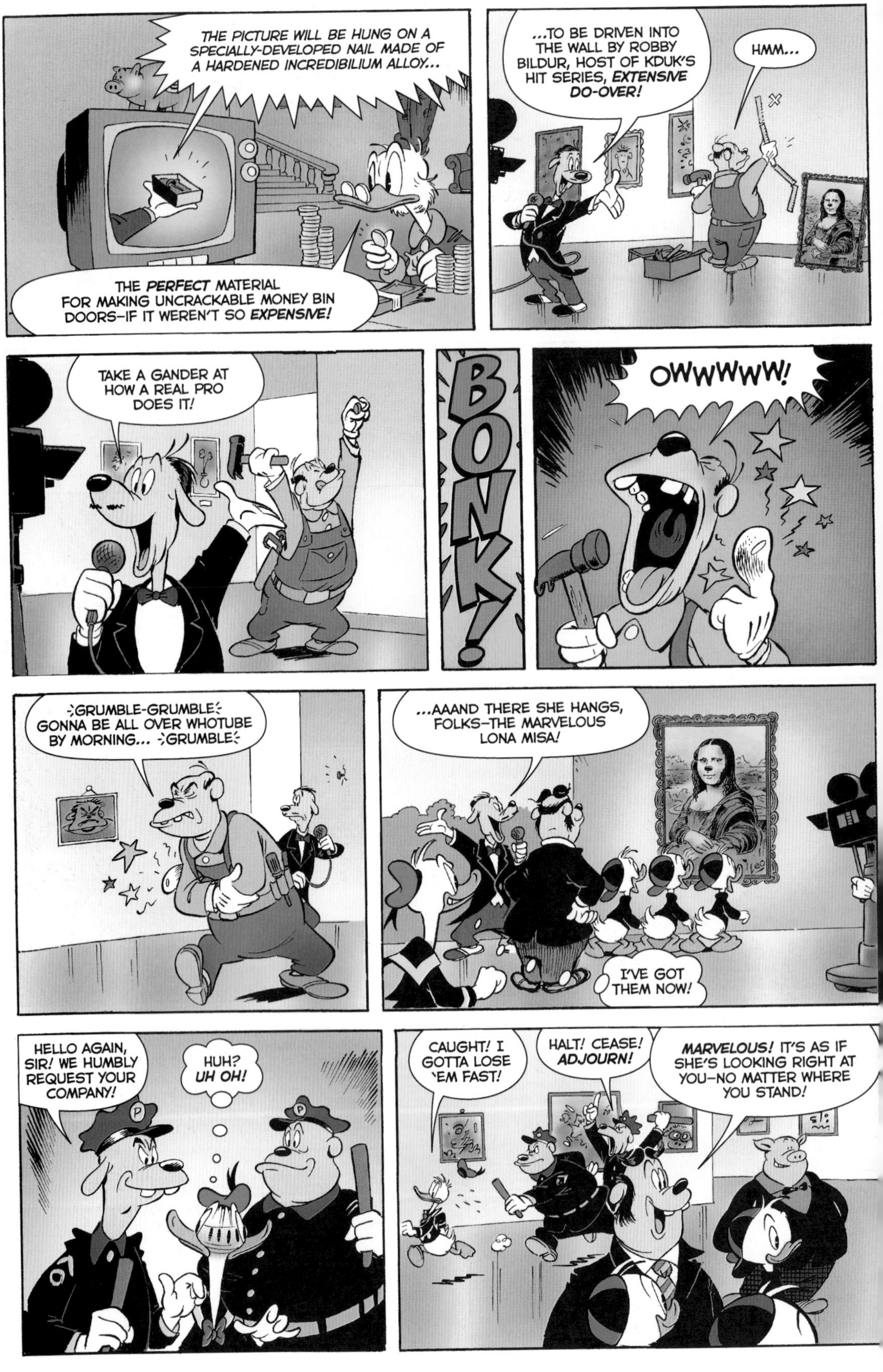

THE PICTURE WILL BE HUNG ON A SPECIALLY-DEVELOPED NAIL MADE OF A HARDENED INCREDIBILIUM ALLOY...
THE *PERFECT* MATERIAL FOR MAKING UNCRACKABLE MONEY BIN DOORS—IF IT WEREN'T SO *EXPENSIVE!*
...TO BE DRIVEN INTO THE WALL BY ROBBY BILDUR, HOST OF KDUK'S HIT SERIES, *EXTENSIVE DO-OVER!*
HMM...
TAKE A GANDER AT HOW A REAL PRO DOES IT!
BONK!
OWWWWW!
GRUMBLE-GRUMBLE GONNA BE ALL OVER WHOTUBE BY MORNING... GRUMBLE
...AAAND THERE SHE HANGS, FOLKS—THE MARVELOUS LONA MISA!
I'VE GOT THEM NOW!
HELLO AGAIN, SIR! WE HUMBLY REQUEST YOUR COMPANY!
HUH? *UH OH!*
CAUGHT! I GOTTA LOSE 'EM FAST!
HALT! CEASE! *ADJOURN!*
MARVELOUS! IT'S AS IF SHE'S LOOKING RIGHT AT YOU—NO MATTER WHERE YOU STAND!

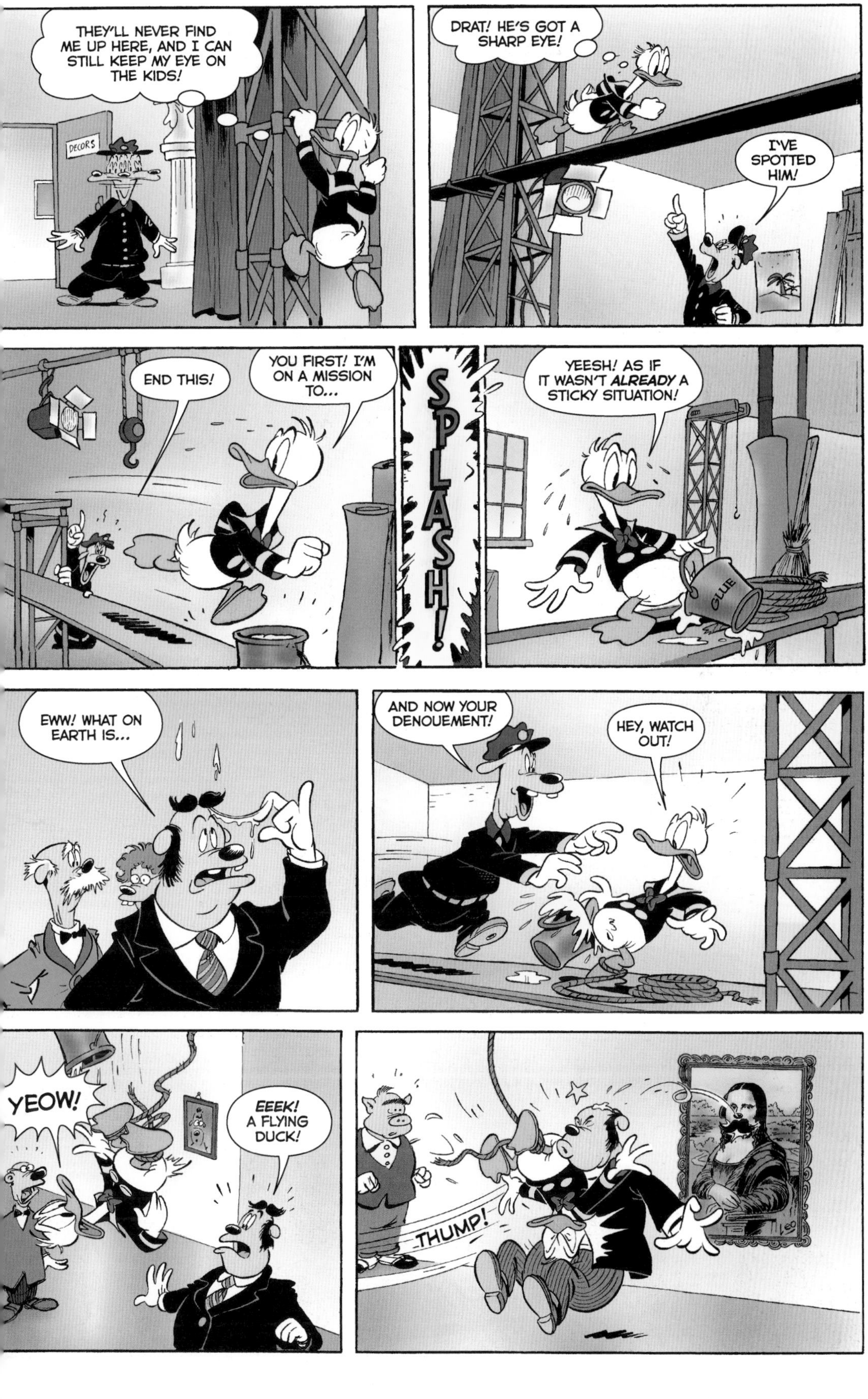
THEY'LL NEVER FIND ME UP HERE, AND I CAN STILL KEEP MY EYE ON THE KIDS!
DECORS
DRAT! HE'S GOT A SHARP EYE!
I'VE SPOTTED HIM!
END THIS!
YOU FIRST! I'M ON A MISSION TO...
SPLASH!
YEESH! AS IF IT WASN'T ALREADY A STICKY SITUATION!
GLUE
EWW! WHAT ON EARTH IS...
AND NOW YOUR DENOUEMENT!
HEY, WATCH OUT!
YEOW!
EEEK! A FLYING DUCK!
THUMP!
LEO

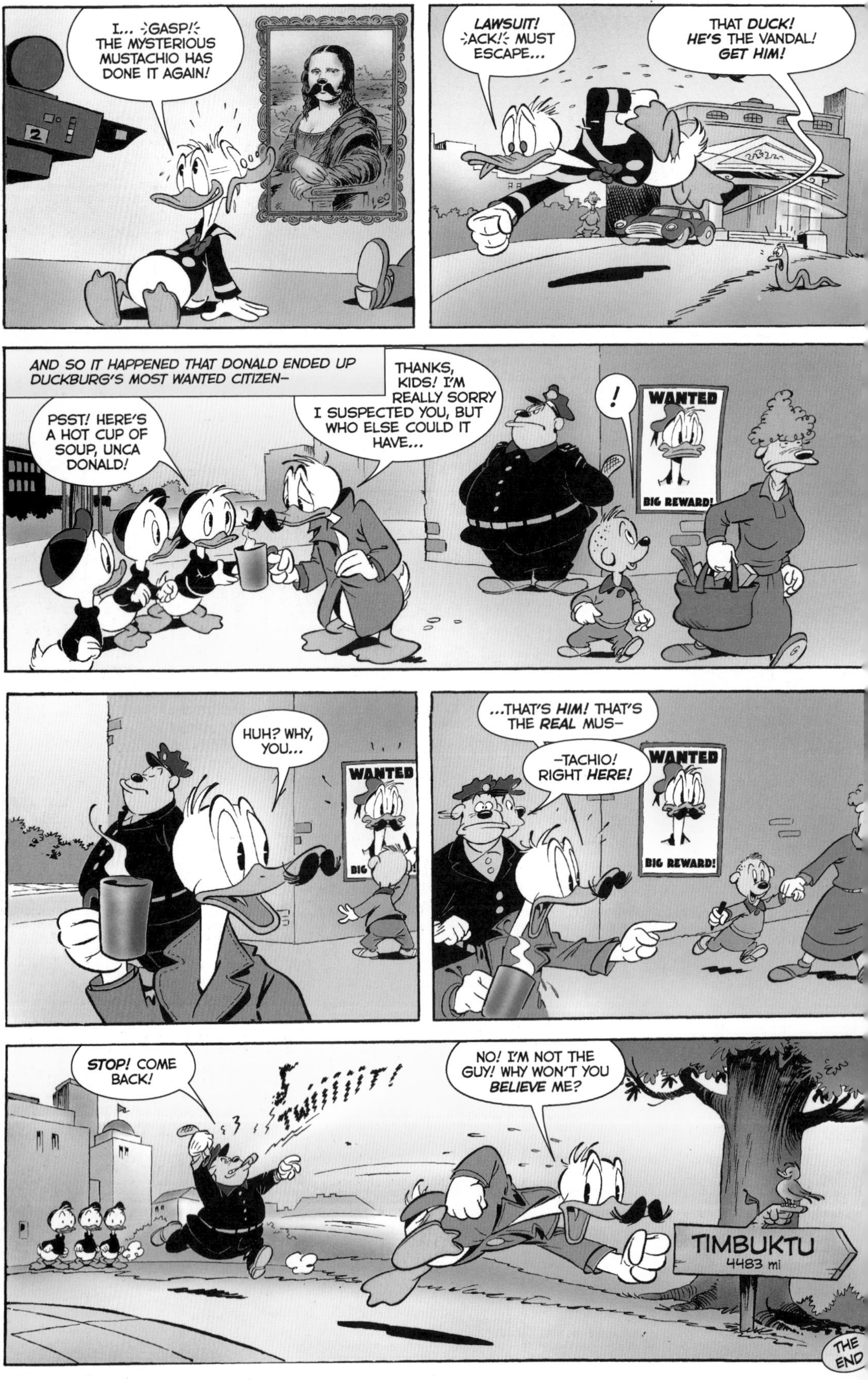
I... GASP! THE MYSTERIOUS MUSTACHIO HAS DONE IT AGAIN!
LAWSUIT! ACK! MUST ESCAPE...
THAT DUCK! HE'S THE VANDAL! GET HIM!
AND SO IT HAPPENED THAT DONALD ENDED UP DUCKBURG'S MOST WANTED CITIZEN—
PSST! HERE'S A HOT CUP OF SOUP, UNCA DONALD!
THANKS, KIDS! I'M REALLY SORRY I SUSPECTED YOU, BUT WHO ELSE COULD IT HAVE...
!
WANTED
BIG REWARD!
HUH? WHY, YOU...
WANTED
...THAT'S HIM! THAT'S THE REAL MUS—
—TACHIO! RIGHT HERE!
WANTED
BIG REWARD!
STOP! COME BACK!
TWIIIIIIT!
NO! I'M NOT THE GUY! WHY WON'T YOU BELIEVE ME?
TIMBUKTU
4483 mi
THE END